"How do you know he followed you?"

"I heard footsteps." Ruby's voice broke.

Jade-green eyes blinked at him with fear in their depths.

Galen felt his heart twist. Part of him had been eager to see Ruby ever since he'd heard she'd stepped in to fill the role of Anastasia's assistant, as the talented princess designed all the jewelry for the upcoming royal weddings. An equal part of him had been wary of a potentially awkward reunion. But awkwardness had become the least of his concerns.

"Are you okay?" He spotted the red marks along her neck where the strap of her bag had cut against her. "Did he hurt you?"

"I'm fine, I think." She touched her neck. "Just sore."

He ignored the way he felt sitting close to her and focused on the attack.

He had things to do—such as reporting the incident to royal guard headquarters and making sure Ruby really was all right.

And figuring out who her attacker was, and what he was after. And then, making sure the man never hurt Ruby again.

Books by Rachelle McCalla

Love Inspired Suspense

Survival Instinct
Troubled Waters
Out on a Limb
Danger on Her Doorstep
Dead Reckoning
*Princess in Peril
*Protecting the Princess
The Detective's Secret Daughter
*Prince Incognito
*The Missing Monarch
†Defending the Duchess
†Royal Heist

*Reclaiming the Crown
†Protecting the Crown

Love Inspired Historical

†A Royal Marriage

RACHELLE McCALLA

is a mild-mannered housewife, and the toughest she ever has to get is when she's trying to keep her four kids quiet in church. Though she often gets in over her head, as her characters do, and has to find a way out, her adventures have more to do with sorting out the carpool and providing food for the potluck. She's never been arrested, gotten in a fistfight or been shot at. And she'd like to keep it that way! For recipes, fun background notes on the places and characters in this book and more information on forthcoming titles, visit www.rachellemccalla.com.

ROYAL HEIST

RACHELLE MCCALLA

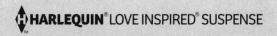
HARLEQUIN® LOVE INSPIRED® SUSPENSE

Recycling programs
for this product may
not exist in your area.

 ™ LOVE INSPIRED BOOKS

ISBN-13: 978-0-373-44545-5

ROYAL HEIST

Copyright © 2013 by Rachelle McCalla

Printed in U.S.A.

Lift up your eyes and look to the heavens:
Who created all these?
He who brings out the starry host one by one
and calls forth each of them by name.
Because of his great power and mighty strength,
not one of them is missing.
—*Isaiah* 40:26

Do not store up for yourselves treasures on earth,
where moths and vermin destroy,
and where thieves break in and steal.
But store up for yourselves treasures in heaven,
where moths and vermin do not destroy, and where
thieves do not break in and steal. For where your
treasure is, there your heart will be also.
—*Matthew* 6:19–21

To Eddie and Ginger McCalla. Thank you for raising your son to be an honorable and Godly man.

ONE

Ruby Tate looked over her shoulder at the sound of footsteps behind her.

A hulking figure, more shadow than man, slipped behind the nearest building.

Ruby blinked. Was someone there, or were her eyes playing tricks on her in the dimness of dusk? Unsure of how to react, Ruby walked faster. At the end of the block she turned the corner. The road bent uphill toward the Lydian royal palace. She would soon put the empty street behind her.

Footfalls echoed behind her again—moving faster now.

Ruby increased her pace to a trot. She had two blocks left to reach the door to her apartment building, built into the rear wall of the palace grounds.

The looming sounds behind her picked up their pace, as well. Was it her imagination, or was he gaining on her?

Ruby ran. She gripped her purse with one hand to keep it from thumping against her hip as she accelerated to a sprint. She could still hear the resounding proof—louder and faster—that she was not alone.

Risking another backward glance, Ruby saw nothing.

No one.

She slowed, looking back again, this time scanning the street for the source of the noise she was nearly certain she still heard.

Where had the man gone? Ruby panted, catching her breath, thinking quickly. Was someone actually chasing her? In all the times she'd visited the Mediterranean kingdom of Lydia with Princess Stasi years before, while the two of them were roommates studying gemology in the United States, Ruby had never heard of any violent crimes in the Christian monarchy. She and Stasi had been out late and walked the city streets, without incident, far more times than she could count.

The memories stilled her fear. In those days, Princess Stasi had a bodyguard named Galen, a youngish guard with a lopsided smile, who'd acted as much as an accomplice as a guard, helping them sneak back inside the palace when Stasi had missed her curfew, keeping Stasi's identity under wraps so they could mingle anonymously with the locals.

But everything had changed in the last year. In June, a fiery ambush against the royal family had shattered the peace of the tiny kingdom. And Ruby hadn't spoken to Galen since their painful parting the previous summer.

A noise startled her.

Were those footsteps again?

Ruby wasn't about to stick around to find out. She sprinted toward the safety of the palace, her ballet flats slamming against the cobblestones as she glanced between buildings, looking for the source of the sounds. Between her rushed breathing and the distant traffic noise from a busy thoroughfare several blocks away, Ruby couldn't be sure what she heard.

But it sounded like the footsteps were drawing nearer again.

With one long block to go, Ruby passed the break of a side street, glancing down the branching road in time to see a large man tearing toward her from the shadows. Something covered his face—a sheer mesh, like nylon stockings, distorting his features into those of a hideous monster.

The man had her cut off. If she ran straight for her apartment door, she'd run right into his path. He'd be on her in seconds.

Ruby nearly stumbled as she changed direction, taking the other branch of the cross street at a dead sprint, the heavy footsteps closing in.

She cut down an alley. She'd taken this path with Stasi years before. There was a pedestrian gate just ahead that led through the palace wall, with a gatehouse manned by royal guards.

Royal guards meant safety—if she could stay ahead of her pursuer long enough to reach them.

Thick boots hammered the cobblestones directly behind her. He was close, far too close. She could hear each rasping breath as the man panted in her wake. The palace wall was near but still too far away.

Something tugged at her hair. Fingers swiped her arm, grasping at her shirt.

She was never going to make it. The pedestrian gate lay a full twenty yards ahead, already within view, but rough hands closed over her arms, breaking her flight and tugging her backward.

Ruby let out a panicked scream a split second before a hand slipped over her mouth.

"What was that?" Galen Harris asked.

"Eh?" Elias, whose guard shift had ended half an hour before, lingered in the pedestrian gate guardhouse, chatting as he so often did.

"It sounded like a scream."

Ever since Princess Anastasia had called ten minutes before, asking him to watch for her assistant Ruby's return, Galen had kept his attention on the security screen, which he'd switched to show the area outside Ruby's apartment door. There'd been no sign of the princess's friend.

Not out back, anyway. The scream had come from down

the block, beyond the scope of the security camera. Galen peered out the rear window and caught sight of two figures struggling in the distant darkness.

"Watch the guardhouse!" Galen punched the button that unlocked the door. He burst out as the woman screamed again, the sound muffled. The evening's dying light glinted off her red hair.

Ruby.

Galen bounded through the door. He'd heard she was in town, and wondered if Ruby would let him see her again after the way her visit had ended the previous summer. Certain his company wasn't welcome, he'd purposely avoided her.

But he couldn't stay away now.

"Halt!" he shouted. "Royal guard!"

The attacker glanced up, his features marred by nylon netting. He moved his hand from Ruby's mouth only to grab her by the arms.

Galen tore toward them. The masked man tugged at Ruby's purse strap, shoving against her shoulder with his other hand as he wrenched at the bag.

With a leap, Galen threw himself at the hefty brute, slamming his arm down on the hand that gripped Ruby's purse strap.

The man's grasp broke as he stumbled backward, still standing, even with Galen half on top of him.

"Run to the gate!" Galen shouted to Ruby as he attempted to restrain her attacker. The thug spun on his heels to run, but Galen didn't want the mugger running free on the streets of Sardis, Lydia's capital city. He grabbed the man by the arm, pulling him back.

Behind them, he heard the faint buzz that meant Elias had deactivated the electronic lock on the door so that Ruby could get inside. Relieved that she was safe, Galen turned all his attention to the angry man in front of him.

Tugging hard on his arm, Galen tried to bring him down, but his massive opponent spun his arm toward Galen's neck.

Galen saw the blow coming a split-second before it hit him and ducked to take the blow with his hard forehead instead of his neck.

The man grunted as his fingers crunched against Galen's skull.

Taking advantage of the man's momentary weakness, Galen threw his weight against him, heaving downward on his arm. But in spite of his strength and skill as a fighter, Galen was outweighed by Ruby's attacker who resisted his downward pull.

Changing tactics, Galen jabbed one heavy boot toward the middle of the man's legs, hoping to knock his knees out from under him. The thug pulled away, clear of Galen's kicks.

Galen lunged onto the man's back, determined to bring him down. The attacker sagged, but snapped one arm over his shoulder toward Galen's face. This time his opponent angled his fist deeper and caught Galen full on the nose, snapping his head backward and sending tears to his eyes, momentarily stunning him.

Before Galen could pull him in again, the assailant dived toward the alleyway and fled into the night.

A gush of blood flooded from Galen's throbbing nostrils. He squinted after the man, but his vision was blurred with tears and he could hardly see where the attacker had gone.

"Galen?" A female gasped behind him.

"Get inside." He gestured to Ruby, who'd stepped back outside and now hovered anxiously near the gate.

She ducked back into the guard booth. As Galen staggered back to the brightly lit doorway, she reappeared with a towel in her hands. "Here." She reached toward his bleeding nose.

"I've got it." Galen accepted the towel but insisted on holding it himself, gingerly prodding the bridge of his nose; at least the thug hadn't broken it.

"Sit down." Ruby led him toward the chair where he'd been sitting until he'd heard her scream.

"Who was that guy?" Galen tried to look Ruby in the eye, but the fat towel clamped over his nose blocked most of his vision.

"I don't know. Did you recognize him?"

"No. Where'd he come from?"

"The streets. He followed me, I think from as far as Stasi's studio."

"Followed you?" The words hit him harder than the blow to his nose. It was one thing to have Ruby attacked by a vicious purse-snatcher. It was far worse to think the man had tailed her, targeting her specifically. "How do you know he followed you?"

"I heard footsteps." Ruby's voice broke.

Galen angled his head and adjusted the towel so that he could see her face. He might not stanch the flow of blood as quickly with his head down instead of up, but he needed to see her. He needed to know whether she was okay.

Jade-green eyes blinked at him with fear in their depths.

Galen felt his heart twist. Part of him had been eager to see Ruby ever since he'd heard she'd stepped in to fill the role of Anastasia's assistant, as the talented princess designed all the jewelry for the upcoming royal weddings. An equal part of him had been wary of a potentially awkward reunion. But awkwardness had become the least of his concerns.

"Are you okay?" He spotted the red marks along her neck where the strap of her bag had cut against her. "Did he hurt you?"

"I'm fine, I think." She touched her neck. "Just sore."

Elias, who'd been hovering silently, his attention divided between the two of them and the security screens, reached for the small fridge where the gateway guards kept their lunches and beverages. "Put something cold on that," the older guard suggested, placing a chilled soda in her hands.

Ruby held the bottle like an ice pack against her neck. "Thank you. That helps."

Relieved that she wasn't seriously injured, Galen went back to wondering why the young American had been followed. "He wanted your purse?"

"Did he?" Ruby gingerly touched the red mark left behind when her attacker had tugged on her purse. "I didn't think I made an obvious target, but I guess by walking home alone..." Her words broke off again, and she took a couple slow breaths, meeting his eyes over the towel he held clenched to his nose.

"You weren't an obvious target," Galen reassured her, trying not to think about the way her shining eyes made his heart leap or how much he'd missed seeing her since the last time she'd visited Lydia. Ruby was heir to an American jewelry chain. He was a humble sentinel with the Lydian royal guard. Their lives were worlds apart. She'd pushed him away when he'd tried to overlook their differences before. He ignored the way he felt sitting close to her, and focused on the attack. "If that man wanted to snatch a random bag, he could have gone downtown. Plenty of women don't guard their purses very well when they go out on the town."

Ruby's freckles scrunched slightly as she wrinkled her nose, visibly fighting back her emotions in order to speak. "But why would he want my bag?" She broke his gaze and turned her head away.

"Are you carrying many valuables?"

"Hardly. Not much cash, a debit card, but my bank account is nearly empty already." She opened her purse and took a quick inventory, rifling through papers and receipts. "Lip balm, keys, cheap sunglasses—which are now broken." Ruby's voice faltered as she pulled out the ruined eyewear. The shades had snapped along one rim. A lens fell out as she lifted them.

Galen reached for the fallen lens, then quickly pulled his hand back as Ruby bent to pick it up, as well.

Best to give the pretty redhead her space. That's what she'd asked him for the year before, and he wasn't about to push the issue. He had things to do—like reporting the incident to royal guard headquarters, and making sure Ruby really was all right.

And figuring out who her attacker was, and what he was after. And then, making sure the man never hurt Ruby again.

TWO

Ruby nearly dropped the broken sunglasses before she got them back into her purse. Maybe she could fix them.

Just like all the other things in her life that needed fixing right now. She'd come to Lydia at Princess Anastasia's invitation. Her best friend from gemology school had set the ambitious goal of designing unique jewelry for the many upcoming Lydian royal weddings, starting with the marriage of Princess Isabelle and Levi Grenaldo in just over a week.

Those pieces were ready to go, but Stasi and Ruby still worked long hours trying to meet the deadlines that lay ahead, which was why Ruby hadn't left the studio until twilight. Ruby was thrilled to help the princess. More than that, she felt honored that Stasi had given her family's line of jewelry stores, Tate Jewelry, exclusive reproduction rights to all the designs.

Given the level of public interest in the royal weddings, the Tate Jewelry reproductions should sell well. Maybe even well enough to save the family business. But Ruby had a lot of work ahead of her if that was going to happen. She didn't need the interference of an attacker to set her even further behind. If Galen hadn't come to her aid, she might be as broken as the sunglasses in her purse.

Horrified that Galen had been hurt while helping her, Ruby turned away from the sight of the injured guard. It was hard

enough for her to be near him at all. Seeing him hurt, remembering how much she cared for him...it was too much to think
about, especially in the wake of what happened.

Ruby stared through the street-side window at the crime
site, a mere dozen yards away, where she'd struggled against
the masked man. Galen's blood had splashed on the cobblestones, marking the spot. Her heart pinched at the sight.

Galen Harris.

She'd purposely avoided him since she'd been back in
Lydia because of her embarrassing last encounter with him
the previous summer and her feelings toward him that had
made their final parting so awkward. She'd made up her mind
that she needed to keep her distance from him, but telling
him so had proven catastrophic.

It wasn't that she didn't enjoy his company. It was precisely
the opposite. The man could distract her from anything, even
her goal of saving her parents' business, which she must do to
earn back their trust after her accidental betrayal years before.

If she revived her friendship with Galen, she didn't know
if she could leave Lydia again. The tiny Christian kingdom
was her favorite place in the world, not just because of the
friendly people and perfect climate, but because of the fasci-
nating history of the place. The kingdom of Lydia could trace
its history all the way back to the days of the Bible. The kingdom was named after the woman whose house church had
grown into a small, independent nation. Princess Stasi and
the rest of the Lydian royal family could trace their lineage
all the way back to Lydia, the dealer in purple cloth who appeared in Acts 16: 14 & 40.

Ruby wasn't sure which was more difficult—leaving Lydia
or leaving Galen. One glance at the guard stirred her dor-
mant feelings back to life. His ready smile was irresistible.
His dark hair, now cropped to military shortness, curled as
it grew out, ready to burst forth like his fun-loving nature
the moment it escaped the rigid parameters around him. But

given the way she'd left things with him the year before, she doubted he'd want to be friends anymore, anyway.

Rather than think about Galen, Ruby focused on the cobblestones outside and tried to sort out what had happened.

Why had that awful man attacked her? The brute had obviously planned ahead—he'd brought whatever that was that he'd put on to disguise his face. Ruby shuddered at the memory of the man's fearsome appearance.

He'd looked warped—grotesque, even. And yet, Ruby couldn't shake the feeling that she'd seen him before somewhere. She tried to recall his features. His nose had seemed large, but then again, maybe that was because the mesh had flattened it. His hair had been...pale.

She wanted to remember more, but the one thing that stuck with her was the lingering sense of recognition. In spite of the distorting effects of his mask, there was something familiar about him. Unsettling, but still, familiar.

She couldn't place it. Maybe it would come to her.

"I think the bleeding's stopped." Galen sniffed a few times as if to be sure.

Ruby turned to face him, saddened that his lopsided smile had been erased by the attack. His bushy eyebrows—which bent stubbornly downward and gave him a sad-eyed teddy bear look—were ruffled, swelling upward from a bruise already forming on his forehead.

Her heart wrenched with concern, but she managed to keep her voice level. "Thank you for saving me."

Galen opened his mouth, looked as though he was about to protest, to say that he hadn't saved her at all, but then he nodded. "I'm just glad I heard you scream."

She thought perhaps he might say more, even wished he'd bring up their awkward parting so she could apologize, though she dreaded having such a conversation. Instead he turned to face a bank of monitors, clicked a few keys on a keyboard, and a moment later, one of the screens showed the scene just outside the window.

"I'm going to back up the security footage and review what happened," Galen explained gently. "I was watching the view of your apartment door when the attack occurred, so I haven't seen what this camera recorded. I understand if you don't want to watch, but it might be helpful—"

"I want to." Ruby surprised herself with the conviction in her voice, and Galen's eyebrows went up. "Maybe I'll recognize him." To her relief, Galen didn't ask any more questions. He simply reversed the footage to the point when she came running into view.

At the sight of her own terrified face, Ruby wasn't so sure if she should have insisted on viewing the replay after all. But her attacker appeared on the shadowy periphery a moment later, pulling her back until they struggled just beyond the scope of the security camera, their feet darting on and off the edge of the screen.

The screen showed Galen clearly as he ran to her aid and Ruby shuffling backward toward the gatehouse. "Not a single image," Galen muttered as he clicked back to the moment when the attacker had rushed her, head down, and pulled her from the camera's view.

"It's as if he knew the range of the camera," Ruby whispered.

"It wouldn't be hard for him to guess if he had scoped out the palace wall ahead of time. The cameras are in clear view to deter trespassers." Galen reviewed the scene again, this time zooming in toward the man's head. The high-resolution image stayed crisp, but it still didn't help much. "I can see the top of his head under his nylon, but I can't even see if the man has hair or not."

"And we can't see any of his face." Ruby realized she'd bent down and taken hold of the back of Galen's chair as he sat using the security computer. When he swung his chair around, suddenly their faces were quite close.

She pulled away a reluctant second too late. She'd seen more than she wanted to of the swelling bruises on Galen's face. She'd met his eyes long enough to feel the latent connection, to know in the bittersweet pit of her heart that he remembered all the time they'd spent together, that he wondered where they stood now.

What could she tell him? *I'm sorry.* The words burned in her throat, unspoken.

"Are you going to report this incident to headquarters?" Elias asked.

"Right away," Galen assured the older guard. "I was just hoping to have an image to send along with my report."

"I should head back to my apartment and get out of your way." Ruby took a step toward the door.

"Wait." Galen stood. He raised one hand as though to reach for her, then returned his arm quickly to his side. "Do you want someone to walk you home?"

Ruby felt her heart swell with a mixture of regret and appreciation. Even though she was within the protective walls of the palace grounds, beyond the reach of the man who'd attacked her and run away, she still hadn't been keen on stepping out into the darkness alone. How thoughtful of Galen to consider her feelings.

Before she could muster up words, Elias stepped forward. "I can walk her home. You've got a call to put in and a gatehouse to keep secure. I'm off duty."

"That's right." Galen looked the tiniest bit disappointed as he accepted Elias's offer. "Thank you."

And though Ruby felt grateful for the older guard's willingness to see that she arrived back at her apartment safely, she couldn't help feeling the slightest bit disappointed, too. She told herself it was simply because she'd hoped for another opportunity to thank Galen, but her heart wouldn't believe it.

She *wanted* him to walk her home, though she dreaded discussing the way they'd left things, and she'd told herself a thousand times to keep her distance. It was precisely the reminder she needed. Galen was a distraction she couldn't afford, not with all the long hours of hard work that lay ahead of her, both in Lydia and back in the US. Perhaps it was best to leave things at that.

"Thank you," she whispered, the words inadequate after the blows he'd taken on her behalf.

"Just doing my job." He kept his face to the screen, but she glanced back to find him looking after her, too far away now for her to read his expression. She might have thought she saw a glimmer of longing, but it was surely just a trick of the light.

"You abandoned your post." Jason Selini, the captain of the Lydian Royal Guard, glared at Galen.

"That guy was going to carry off Princess Anastasia's assistant. Besides, Elias had the gatehouse covered." Galen wished the royal guard had enough men to have two guards posted at the gatehouse at all hours, but following the attack on the royal family at the beginning of the summer, they'd had to let go any guard with ties to the insurgents. Rebuilding the force would take time.

"Elias was off duty. You should have called for backup."

"And waited while that man—"

"Guards could have arrived in under a minute. If that attack had been a ruse to draw you away from your post, you fell for it. You left the whole palace vulnerable." Captain Selini flopped a file open on his desk.

Galen recognized the pages with a sinking heart.

"Last month," the captain continued, "you let Duchess Julia through the gate without a guard. You have breached protocol twice in less than a month. That alone is grounds for suspension."

Galen felt as though a cold hand had clenched him in its

grasp. He wanted to protest, but the captain clearly wasn't going to listen to his defense.

"In light of the events of last evening, Princess Anastasia has requested an evening escort for her assistant. She specifically requested *you*." Selini raised a skeptical eyebrow. "Do you have any idea why?"

"Because I fought Ruby's attacker?"

"Because you and Ruby have a history together, according to the princess. I looked into this history." Selini flipped back several pages in his file.

Galen's heart sank. He knew what those pages held. During the tenure of the former head of the royal guard, Galen's infractions hadn't been considered much of a concern. But the former captain had been engaged in the treasonous conspiracies that had led to an ambush on the royal family, and had nearly toppled the monarchy. Jason Selini had taken the traitor's place and seemed determined to restore the royal guard to its former glory by wiping away every trace of misbehavior.

"It seems two years ago," the captain summarized from the report, "you made an unauthorized journey to the archipelago in a royal guard motorboat with the princess and her friend at night."

Galen recalled the event distinctly. Princess Stasi had wanted to watch a meteor shower far away from the lights of Sardis. Galen's plan to borrow the boat would have worked perfectly if only the engine hadn't refused to start when they'd tried to head home. After attempting to row back to the marina with little success, he'd ended up tying a rope from his waist to the prow and swimming back to shore, tugging the disabled craft behind him. They'd arrived at the dock shortly after daybreak, an hour after the boat was reported stolen.

The former head of the guard had laughed heartily when Galen had explained the story.

His new boss didn't laugh. "Compounded with your recent infractions, these reports provide sound basis for your immediate dismissal."

Galen couldn't speak. Would he really lose his job? Jason Selini, appointed in the wake of the ambush in June, had terminated any and every guard who'd been linked to those who'd conspired against the Royal House of Lydia, determined to defend the royal family even from those hired to protect them.

Captain Selini obviously had no qualms about firing guards. And while Galen had wholeheartedly supported his boss's decisions—supported every move that would restore the royal guard to its former glory—he hadn't expected the captain's zealous housecleaning to threaten his job.

Selini ran his hands through his thick hair, revealing a few gray roots that had sprung up in recent months. His face, too, had lost its former easygoing expression, replaced with a stern grimness impressed by the weight of his newfound responsibilities. "I've got six new recruits scheduled to start in two weeks, as soon as they can be officially transferred over from the Lydian army. I can't afford to let you go just yet. You have two weeks left."

With a pounding heart, Galen listened to his supervisor's words, waiting for the final verdict. The treason among the ranks of the guard had dealt a horrific blow to their prestige. Galen's own brothers ribbed him mercilessly for wearing the same uniform as those who'd tried to overthrow the monarchy. Galen had vowed to help reclaim the royal guard's reputation.

He couldn't do that if the captain fired him.

How could he ever face his older brothers if he lost his job? His family had served in the Lydian military for generations. His brothers were all men of rank. After serving four years in the Lydian Army, Galen had become a guard—in part to escape his brothers' constant scrutiny and the reminder that he could never measure up.

If he was fired from the guard, he'd never be able to show his face at a family gathering again. Worse yet, he wouldn't be a part of the guard he wanted to help restore.

The captain glared at Galen as he continued. "For the next two weeks, I'll be keeping close tabs on everything you do and every choice you make. If, at the end of that time, I determine that these protocol lapses are typical of your judgment, then you will be terminated. However, if you can prove to me that you have what it takes to be a royal guard, then you can keep your job. Agreed?"

Galen nearly sagged with relief, and panted to catch the breath he'd been holding the entire time Selini had spoken. "Agreed. Thank you. You won't be sorry."

"I hope not." The captain closed the file and rapped the pages against the desk like the blade of a guillotine slamming down. "Now, Princess Anastasia wants a royal guard escort for her assistant every evening on her way home from work. She's specifically requested you for the job. I'm not thrilled with her selection given your record, but since we don't have a decent picture of her attacker, and since you're the only guard who's actually seen the man, you're the obvious choice."

Still feeling exhilarated by the news that he hadn't yet been terminated, Galen smiled giddily at the thought of spending more time with Ruby. "Yes, thank you."

If anything, his boss appeared concerned by Galen's response. He leaned across his desk, and his eyes, already glaring, narrowed to dark slits. "Are you certain you can handle that?"

Galen sobered immediately. "Yes."

"Quite certain?" Selini didn't look convinced.

"Quite certain," Galen assured his superior officer.

It wasn't until he'd been dismissed and made it halfway down the hall that he realized maybe he wasn't after all. Could he handle walking Ruby home for the next two weeks, with

Jason Selini scrutinizing his every move, ready to dismiss him for the slightest infraction?

He wasn't sure which was more worrisome—the man who'd attacked Ruby, or the thought of trying to maintain protocol while in her very distracting presence. He'd felt their old connection from the moment he'd looked into her eyes the previous evening. If it hadn't been for her cold request the summer before, Galen might have acted on those feelings.

As he'd promised Captain Selini, could he handle walking Ruby home? From a professional standpoint, it shouldn't be difficult. He was a trained royal guard. He knew what he was doing. But what about the woman who could make him lose his head with a single look? Suddenly he wasn't so certain at all.

The evening after the attack, Ruby was alone at the studio after everyone else had left for. She looked up from the table where she sat sorting gemstones into precise piles by color and size and she startled.

A broad-shouldered figure loomed in the doorway across the room. Shoving the magnifying goggles high onto her forehead, she blinked at the figure.

"Galen!" She gasped in relief when she recognized him. "I didn't realize anyone else was here."

"Kirk and the princess let me in as they left. I thought they'd told you I'd be stopping by to escort you home," Galen explained. Kirk Covington, Princess Stasi's fiancé, had been a sentinel with the royal guard for years before saving Stasi's life and being assigned as her primary guard.

"Stasi mentioned that she'd requested a guard, but she didn't say who it would be." Ruby peeled off the goggles and placed them on the table.

"I'm the only one who saw the man who attacked you." Galen shrugged, his words an excuse for his presence.

Ruby still felt the urge to argue against it. "I caught a

glimpse of him, too." She stretched her arms above her head, releasing the kink that had built up in her neck over the course of the many hours she'd spent hunched over her work. "But that doesn't mean I'd recognize him unless he came at me with panty hose over his face again."

"I hope that doesn't happen, but if he shows up again, at least you won't be alone this time." Galen glanced around the studio. "Are you ready to head home?"

"Not just yet, if you don't mind. If I don't seal these stones into separate containers, someone could bump the table and my entire evening's work could be lost." She picked up the first container. "It won't take me more than ten minutes."

"Take your time. I'm going to walk the perimeter."

"Great idea. Kirk does the same thing several times a day." Ruby returned her attention to the task before her, making precise notations on each container to identify the contents.

Absorbed by her task, Ruby had almost managed to stop thinking about Galen's presence when he called out to her from across the room, "Ruby? I need you to come over here, but stay down, out of sight from the windows."

THREE

Ruby felt awkward as she crawled on her hands and knees across the varnished wooden floorboards toward the second story window. Ahead of her, Galen crouched to the side of the expansive glass panes, hidden from outside view by the wide limestone window casing.

"What is it? Do you see someone?" Ruby asked as she drew slowly nearer.

"There's a man at the corner smoking a cigarette. He's leaning against the building across the street. It could be completely innocent, or he could be waiting for you."

She was almost to the window. "The man who attacked me last night had that lingering scent that smokers have."

"And Lydia has one of the lowest smoking rates on the planet. That doesn't mean he's our man, but it's certainly an implicating factor."

Ruby reached the window. Instead of the cigarette odor they'd been discussing, she caught a whiff of Galen's cologne, a faint but exotic scent that immediately reminded her of the time she'd danced with Galen, two summers before. Her heart began to beat faster as the treasured memory welled up. She tried to put it from her mind and focus on the situation.

"Keep your head just above the windowsill," Galen instructed her. "We're on the second floor and he's at ground level, so he shouldn't be able to see you as long as you stay low."

Ruby slowly lifted her head just high enough to allow her to see out, while Galen crouched down beside her, until they were both peeking out in the same direction. The sun had nearly set, and though electric lights illuminated most of the cobbled streets, the place where the man had chosen to stand was cast almost entirely in shadows.

The only thing Ruby could see clearly was the orange glow of a cigarette. "He's certainly built like the man who came after me last night." Ruby was able to make out enough of the large silhouette to determine that much. "I wish he'd step into the light so we could see his face."

"If he's the same man, I doubt he'll do that. But I'll keep watching. You can finish what you were doing. I just wanted you to get a look before he disappeared."

"Thank you." Ruby met Galen's eyes, aware of how close their hands were, clinging to the windowsill, and how near his face was to hers. An indigo bruise branched out from his nose, deepening to a ruddy purple under his eye. Ruby sucked in a sharp breath. "Your face looks awful."

Galen grinned the lopsided grin she'd missed so much. After an awkward silence in which she tried to think of what to say to clarify what she'd meant, Galen responded, "Yours looks quite the opposite."

Mortified, Ruby dropped to the floor and crawled back toward where she'd been working. Had Galen meant his words to sound flirtatious? She didn't want to know the answer.

Over the course of her many summer visits to Lydia, she'd worked hard to maintain a purely professional relationship with the gorgeous guard. The first summer she'd had a boyfriend back in the US, so she'd made it a point never to act on the attraction she had felt toward Galen. And by the time she'd had a school year away to contemplate the feelings that wouldn't go away, she'd realized that a relationship with Galen would never work.

He was committed to life in Lydia. She had long ago promised her parents she'd help with their chain of jewelry stores once she finished her studies—and that required her to live in the United States. And she'd never been the type to have a casual fling with a man just because he was cute, even if he had sad-teddy-bear eyes. If she couldn't foresee a future together, she didn't see the point of wasting her time and emotional investment in a relationship.

Galen was a great guy; definitely marriage material for some lucky Lydian girl. But Ruby belonged on the other side of the globe. Galen was a friend—a great friend, who'd only ever been a gentleman in the past, in spite of the adventures they'd shared that had given him plenty of opportunity to make a move on her if he'd wanted to. Most likely the amiable sentinel was just trying to be kind.

There was nothing more for her to read into his words. There would never be anything more between them than friendship—their awkward parting the previous summer had surely guaranteed that. She'd hate to mess up what camaraderie they now shared by drawing attention to words he couldn't possibly have meant to sound flirtatious. Even if he felt for her something like what she felt for him, nothing could come from it.

It would be difficult enough for her to leave Lydia when her service to Princess Stasi ended. She didn't think she could leave Galen behind again, not if he felt for her what she felt for him. It was best not to think about those feelings, certainly not to discuss them.

Ruby had solidified her convictions by the time she labeled the last of the tiny containers. "Is he still there?" she asked Galen, who remained crouched at the windowsill where she'd left him.

"I believe so. He stepped back, but I've seen that shadow

move, so I think he's just around the corner. Do you feel comfortable walking home or do you want me to call for a car? I'd have driven myself but—"

"The streets in this part of the old city are too narrow for parking and driving." Ruby understood completely. "The nearest decent parking is in the royal garage. And we don't have very far to go." She pondered the choices before them.

Was the man on the corner the same person who'd come after her the night before? She had no way of knowing, not unless he tried to come after her again. And until they caught whoever had attacked her, she would never know when he might be lurking behind her. Perhaps it would be best to give him a chance to show himself. Maybe then her life would return to normal.

"I don't suppose you can ask your fellow guards to sneak up behind this guy and nab him, can you?"

"Sorry." Galen stayed low, out of sight of the window as he shuffled toward her, standing when he reached the table where she'd been working. "He's not breaking any laws right now. We don't have any way to prove it's your attacker. The only way to legally apprehend him is to catch him in the act."

Ruby shuddered as she imagined what that act might be. Grabbing her? Fighting Galen again? What had the man been trying to accomplish, anyway? "Have you got a quick way to call in more men if this guy tries to jump us again?"

"Yes. The head of the guard assigned extra men to this shift in response to last night's attack. There are two men on duty in the guardhouse, and they can call more reinforcements if they need to. I'll call them now and tell them we'll be leaving, so they know to watch for us."

As Ruby listened to Galen's half of the conversation, the guard used his radio earpiece to contact the other men and fill them in on the situation, including the fact that they'd spotted a man across the street. "We haven't gotten a good look at him. Might be our guy. Might not. We should have a better idea in a few minutes."

Galen offered Ruby a focused smile as he ended the conversation. "They'll be watching for us."

Reassured, Ruby did her best to sound confident. "We'll be fine. You fought him off last night. Why would he be crazy enough to show up again? He has to know I won't be walking home alone after what happened. That's probably some innocent man taking a long smoke break." Ruby made up her mind. "Your men are expecting us. Let's just go." She grabbed her pile of notes from that day's work and stuffed them into her purse, strapping it across her chest as usual.

Galen walked with her to the stairwell. "I'll step outside first. Then I'll stand behind you as you close the door. I want you to walk just ahead of me, a little to my right, closest to the buildings. That puts me in between you and anyone who might come from behind."

"Okay. What do we do if he shows up?"

"Let's try to stay together. If I tell you to run, head for your apartment door or the gatehouse like last night. The guards will have one man watching through the window, and one watching the security footage of your door. I'll call for reinforcements if this guy makes any move toward us. If I can, I'd like to bring him in—but not if it means putting you in danger." Galen's gaze settled on hers with a protective expression that bordered on...

No, that couldn't be it. Not affection. Galen knew better. She'd made herself perfectly clear the year before. Even if he felt things for her, she wouldn't believe it.

Couldn't return it.

Mindful of her decision not to let on to him about her feelings, she turned her face to the door. "I'm ready. Let's go."

The night air felt cool on his face as Galen stepped outside. As promised, he took his position just behind Ruby as she bolted the door and slipped the key into her purse. In those brief moments, he turned to get a clear view of where the man had been standing.

The spot was empty. If it hadn't been for the lingering scent of tobacco in the air, Galen might have wondered if he hadn't imagined seeing the shadowy figure. There was no sign of the man anymore.

Ruby turned resolutely toward the palace.

Galen listened carefully as he kept pace half a step behind her. He heard no footsteps, saw no evidence of life.

He exhaled with his mouth half open, not wanting even the sound of his own breath to disguise any sign that Ruby's attacker might be near. Tuning out the distant noises of traffic from several blocks away, Galen listened closely for the faintest footstep.

Nothing.

Good. Though he wanted to catch the man, he didn't want to put Ruby in danger. If he'd thought the guy was crazy enough to show up two nights in a row, he'd have requested more guards with him. But no mere mugger would bother to show up two nights in a row or try to attack a woman surrounded by royal guards. If Galen made such a request only to walk home undisturbed, he'd look foolish. Jason Selini would question his judgment.

No, it was better this way. No extra guards, and no sign of Ruby's attacker.

They turned the corner at the end of the block. The palace lay up ahead, in clear sight. Ruby looked at him over her shoulder and offered him half a smile, hope sparkling in her eyes. She felt it too, then—relief that the man had decided to leave them alone. Maybe Galen's presence had been enough to keep the thug away.

But a few steps later he heard a crunch like gravel under the sole of a boot.

Ruby must have heard it, too. She stiffened and slowed her

pace slightly, as if stalling her steps to hear as much as possible between each footfall.

Galen held his breath, praying silently that Ruby's attacker would stay away.

A few more steps crunched softly behind them.

He turned his head, quickly scouring the street behind them, but saw no one. The sound continued. It seemed to be coming from around the corner, though the echoing effect of the tall stone buildings made it difficult to tell for sure. The man could be anywhere.

Ruby glanced up at him, her green eyes wide.

"Walk faster," he whispered.

She didn't need any encouragement. Galen took three long strides after her before the clear sound of footsteps rounded the corner. One glance over his shoulder told him their disguised attacker had returned.

"Run!" Galen swept one arm around Ruby's waist as he hurried her forward. At the same instant, he clamped down on his push-to-talk button to call the guards to their aid. But as he opened his mouth to speak, his ears were assaulted with a static-filled squeal.

What was wrong with his radio? Galen didn't have time for troubleshooting. Their pursuer was a mere half block behind them, maybe less.

They crossed a bisecting street. Ruby's apartment lay one long block ahead of them. Galen dared to look over his shoulder as they darted across the intersection, hoping to see that they were far enough ahead of the man to safely reach Ruby's apartment. A shadow passed under a streetlight at the corner behind them, disappearing in the other direction.

"Where is he?" Ruby gasped between breaths.

"He's gone."

"What?"

Ruby's steps slowed. Galen, likewise, stopped running to listen. Silence. Had the man given up?

"I think I saw him dart around that corner away from us." Galen shook his head, still listening closely. He heard a distant sound, which might have been footsteps, but it was difficult to tell as he and Ruby both sucked in deep breaths after their panicked run.

"I hear—" Ruby began in a whisper.

But Galen heard it, too, and pulled out his earpiece so he could hear more clearly. The sound of approaching footsteps had returned, but now they seemed to be coming from the side street opposite the corner around which the man had seemed to disappear.

How had the man gotten across the street? Was it some sort of trick, or another person entirely?

Galen formed a plan quickly. He wanted to ID the perp, if possible—but he couldn't let Ruby stay out in the open. A deep alcove beckoned from the doorway of the nearest building.

"In here." Galen nearly lifted Ruby off her feet as he swept her behind the protecting stone enclosure, positioning himself in front of her, ears attuned, one eye peering just past the rim of the stonework.

As he'd suspected, a massive man darted out from around the opposite corner, his face distorted by a semitransparent, tight-fitting elastic garment. The man glanced about as he ran, then skidded to a stop fewer than twenty yards from them.

Galen ducked his head back.

Ruby clung to the light blue shirt of his royal guard uniform, looking up at him from very close range, her expression trusting in spite of the fear that haunted her eyes. This close, he could feel her warmth and smell the light perfume she wore. He turned his attention from her to the street, refusing to think about how it felt to have her practically in his arms.

Ordinarily he'd have backed away, honoring her wishes to keep a formal distance between them. He didn't have that option, not with their pursuer moving toward them as the big man searched out his lost prey.

The doorway where they hid was set back one yard or more from the stonework facade, the decorative archway providing a narrow nook for them to hide, out of sight from anyone looking directly at the building, provided they pressed flat against the adjoining wall.

"He's looking for us," Galen explained, his voice barely a breath as he tried to compress himself as flat as possible against the wall without crushing Ruby. She too shrank back as they listened to the man approach, but Galen could still feel her heartbeat slamming into his.

A gruff voice rumbled from the street. "Where'd they go?" A pause. "Not anymore." A stream of curses was followed by, "Not tonight."

The sound of footsteps faded into the night.

Galen waited a few more tense heartbeats, then peeled himself away from the wall. He needed to distance himself from Ruby, especially since he wanted to pull her into his arms to hold her close and keep her safe. Instead, he looked out into the night. The orange glow of streetlights illumined all that was left of the evening.

"What happened to your guards?" Ruby asked in a tiny whisper. "I thought you were going to call them?"

As she spoke, Galen heard footsteps—this time coming from the direction of the palace wall. He recognized the familiar dark slacks and pale blue shirt of the Lydian guard uniform.

"Linus!" he called out.

The guard turned, relief on his face as Galen stepped from the doorway, pulling Ruby out after him.

"What happened? I was listening for you, but when I checked the radio, all I got was static."

"He must have jammed the system." Galen was still trying to sort out what had happened. "He may have been wearing an earpiece, as well. Even though he appeared to be alone, he was talking to someone."

"An accomplice?" Ruby's voice, sounding small and vulnerable, pulled Galen's attention from his fellow guard to the woman he'd promised to protect.

Galen stared at Ruby as the full impact of her words hit him. It was worse than he'd feared. Not only was someone targeting her specifically, but they weren't working alone.

Cold dread filled Galen as he looked at Ruby's innocent face and wondered what she was up against. He needed to figure it out—quickly, before the men did anything to hurt Ruby.

And he needed to convince his boss that he knew what he was talking about when he requested more men for the next evening, and every evening until these men were caught. And in the meantime, he'd have to stop staring into Ruby's jade-green eyes or he might easily give in to the impulse to pull her close to him.

FOUR

Ruby stepped through the pedestrian gate ahead of the guards and headed toward the royal guard headquarters, a three-story brick building located on the palace grounds across the courtyard from the garages. Before she and the guards reached the building, the vehicle gate opened and a car pulled through.

"That's Kirk's car," Linus noted.

The coupe rolled toward them and Princess Anastasia leaped from the passenger door, rushing at Ruby and embracing her. "Are you okay?"

"I'm fine." Ruby felt grateful for the hug, but embarrassed that her friend had interrupted a rare evening out on her account. "You're supposed to be on a dinner date."

"We hadn't ordered our food yet. I was worried about how you were faring, so I asked Kirk to call the guards. They told us what happened. I feel responsible—you came to Lydia at my invitation, and now you've been attacked twice."

"Only once, technically." Ruby stepped back toward Galen as she explained, "We were chased this evening, but thanks to Galen's quick thinking, the man didn't catch us."

"Unfortunately, we didn't catch him, either," Galen lamented.

"No, but we may have learned a few things." Linus led the way to the royal guard headquarters. "Let's get those observations on record before either of you have time to forget any details."

Kirk and Stasi followed them inside. Once they were all seated around a table in the conference room, Ruby and Galen recounted everything they could recall, from the moment Galen spotted the figure smoking outside the studio. But when they reached the point in the story where Galen had tried to radio for help, Linus stopped to clarify.

"What happened with that transmission? The royal guard has been using these earpieces for three years, ever since they hit the market. They're supposed to be the best of their kind. We've never had a problem before."

Galen shook his head slowly. "I don't know enough about this technology to guess how they did it. Can we call Simon in here?"

Moments later, the royal guard's technology expert for the evening shift stood among them, nodding as Galen recounted the trouble with the earpiece kits.

"It had to have been deliberately jammed," Simon concluded after hearing the facts. "Given that you'd just used it with no trouble, I'd say he waited until his accomplice was chasing you before jamming the signal."

"It had to be an accomplice?" Ruby didn't like the thought of a team working against her using sophisticated equipment—especially when she didn't even know why. "One man couldn't have jammed the signal while chasing us?"

"Highly unlikely. He'd have to have a transmitter tuned to the same frequency as our receiving equipment, with the same type of modulation and enough power to override the signal at the receiver. I can't imagine someone coordinating all that while slipping on a mask and running after the two of you on foot."

Ruby wasn't clear on all the technical specifics Simon had quoted, but she agreed with the guard's conclusion. Which left her with one looming question. "Why are these guys after me? What do I have that is worth so much effort?"

"They came after you two nights in a row, even after I fought one of them last night." Galen looked apologetic for reminding her of the incident as he explained why they had to revisit it. "That tells me that whatever they want, it's urgent. Under any other circumstances, you'd think they'd lay low for a few days in hopes that we'd lower our guard."

"We're *not* going to lower our guard." Princess Anastasia crossed her arms with determination. "I'll talk to the captain of the guard myself if I have to. This issue will have priority status."

"But your sister's wedding is next Saturday," Kirk reminded his fiancée. "I'm certain that's going to remain our top priority."

"That's all the more reason we've got to get to the bottom of this." The petite princess was known for her tenacity. "The guards will need to focus on Isabelle's wedding. These guys need to be stopped before then." She turned her attention to Ruby. "Can you think of any possible reason these guys keep coming after you?"

Ruby squinted her eyes shut, thinking carefully, then shook her head. "Nothing."

"They tried to take your purse last night," Galen reminded her.

"But there's nothing in it worth stealing."

"Can we see?" Stasi requested.

With a shrug, Ruby turned her purse upside down over the table, unceremoniously dumping it out in full view of everyone. Stasi helped her rifle through the sparse contents. "Your keys." She picked through them. "Do you suppose they wanted your keys to break in to the studio?"

"But why go through Ruby for the keys?" Galen asked. "Why not break directly into the studio?"

"We've installed a sophisticated security system," Kirk

noted, "but if they're clever enough to jam our radio signals, you'd think they could circumvent those defenses."

Ruby listened to their conversation with half an ear, her attention already focused on three pages of notebook paper she'd carefully folded and tucked away in her purse before leaving the studio that evening.

Her jewelry design notes from that day's work. She'd been faithfully toting copious notes back to her apartment every evening, accumulating a file of all the details so that Tate Jewelry could make accurate reproductions. The exclusive rights were a precious gift from her friend Stasi. If the replica jewelry sold as well, and Ruby hoped it might, it amounted to Ruby's best hope for saving her parents' business and earning back their trust. The design notes were invaluable to her.

Might they also be valuable to someone else?

Ruby cleared her throat. "What about this?"

"Your design notes?" Stasi's eyes widened as the meaning of Ruby's suggestion sank in. "Do you think my designs are that valuable?"

"Darling." Kirk placed a hand on his fiancée's shoulder. "You always underestimate the value of your work. Your jewelry is highly sought after, and it's sure to become vastly more so with all the media coverage of the upcoming royal weddings."

Stasi blushed at Kirk's assessment.

Galen didn't look convinced. "How would these guys know you had the designs in your purse?"

Ruby and Stasi looked at one another thoughtfully.

"We talk about jewelry all the time," the princess admitted.

"We've talked about the designs in public," Ruby added.

"At lunch the other day—"

"And when we were shopping—"

"Walking home from the studio—"

Linus interrupted them. "I don't think you should discuss the designs in public anymore. But that said, those are just a few pages in your purse. Wouldn't they need the rest of your notes for that information to be useful?"

Ruby nodded.

Galen murmured in a low voice, "I'm not one hundred percent convinced this is what those guys were after."

"Neither am I," Linus agreed.

"But what else could there be?" Ruby had been pondering the question all day, ever since the attack the evening before, but still hadn't come up with an answer.

Nor did anyone else at the table posit an explanation.

After a thoughtful silence, the princess concluded, "The most important thing right now is keeping you safe. I hate to restrict your freedom, but from here on out I don't want you leaving the palace grounds alone."

Ruby nodded solemnly. Other than traveling to and from Stasi's studio, she rarely went anywhere without her friend. And Stasi always had a guard—usually her fiancée, Kirk—at her side. The new imposition wouldn't change much.

"I'm going to look into alternate earpiece communication kits," Simon offered.

"And I want physical stats on this guy," Linus cut in. "If he got close enough to the palace to deduce our radio frequency, he's probably been lurking around. We shouldn't have to wait for him to come after Ruby again—if we know what he looks like, we can nab him the next time he sticks his head up."

To her frustration, Ruby didn't have anything helpful to offer in the way of a physical description. While Galen estimated the man's height and weight, Ruby pinched her eyes shut and visualized the menacing face she'd seen under the elastic mask the night before. She couldn't imagine why she'd thought the man seemed familiar. Where would she have seen him before? Lurking around, as Linus had suggested? Had he been watching her, sticking to the shadows as he had that evening at the studio, his cigarette glowing like a lone orange eye?

The thought made her shudder.

"Are you okay?" Galen asked.

Ruby opened her eyes to see Galen's teddy-bear brows bent upward with concern. He reached for her hand where it rested at the edge of the table, still gripping her notes on Stasi's designs.

She recoiled at the thought that he might hold her hand. She could still feel the embrace of his strong arms around her as they'd hidden from her attacker. Her heart lurched, torn between reaching for him, and the fear of letting herself share any more connection with a man she wouldn't see after her job in Lydia ended.

Galen pulled his hand back, no doubt recalling her request from the year before. Or perhaps he'd never meant to take her hand at all. "You've had a rough couple days."

Ruby shook her head. "I'm okay. I was trying to figure out why the man who attacked me seemed so—" she struggled to speak through the complicated feelings that clogged her thoughts "—familiar." It wasn't quite the right word, but it was the closest thing she could think of.

"Familiar?" The princess repeated the word with alarm. "Do you think you know this guy?"

"I don't know." Ruby wished she could take the word back, even if she didn't know what else to replace it with. "I couldn't really see his face. Maybe I imagined it."

"Familiar how?" Galen quizzed her. "What does he remind you of?"

Though she hated revisiting the fear-filled memory, Ruby closed her eyes again and tried to link the man's image with whatever it was that she felt she recognized. "I don't know," she concluded again, frustrated with the whole business. "I don't know why these guys are after me, or what's so important to them. I'm not sure if I recognize something about that masked man or if I'm just imagining things."

"It's okay." Galen reached out to her with his words, even as he kept his hands at his sides. "You don't have to know. It's our job as the royal guard to keep you safe."

Stasi jumped in. "As Kirk is always reminding me, safety means more than just freedom from injury. It means freedom from indirect harm, as well. Stressing about your own safety is bad for your health. Speaking of, have you had anything for dinner yet?"

"No."

"Neither have we," Kirk reminded Stasi.

"Let's head over to the palace," Stasi suggested. "They've always got something prepared over there." She pulled Ruby to her feet.

"Galen!" Princess Stasi called back from the doorway. "Come on."

Surprised by the invitation, Galen declined. "I'm on duty tonight."

"Which is why you're coming to supper with us. You're in charge of guarding Ruby from now on. You'll need to co-ordinate your schedule with hers."

"I'm a sentinel, not a bodyguard." Galen hated to argue with a member of the royal family, but guarding Ruby around the clock would mean a whole lot more than just walking her home. He'd promised her at the end of the previous summer that he'd keep his distance. How was he supposed to do that if he was at her side all day, every day? He'd been tempted enough to pull her into his arms on the street outside the palace walls earlier, lasting less than an hour before temptation had struck.

Besides, the assignment didn't fit his job description. The royal guard had three distinct positions for non-officers: detectives, bodyguards and sentinels. Galen's job description was all about guarding buildings, vehicles, and by extension, all the people inside them. He wasn't authorized to protect just one person.

"Kirk was a sentinel before he became my bodyguard." Stasi clearly didn't see why the difference would be an issue. "He can explain the differences for you."

"But Captain Selini has to authorize all changes." Galen felt the futility of his defense as he spoke the words. The captain had already assigned Galen to walk Ruby home. Whatever his cautions about protocol, Selini would most likely agree to Princess Anastasia's expanded request.

"He'll authorize it," Stasi assured him, already headed down the hallway, clearly trusting him to follow. "I'm the one who appointed him Captain of the Guard," she added with a laugh.

Galen followed, but he didn't laugh. He couldn't guard Ruby. That would mean spending time with her, watching her smile, hearing her laugh, fighting the urge to beg her not to leave Lydia again. It would mean resisting, every moment of every day, the urge to pull her into his arms, to be close to her as he'd always longed to be. He'd promised Ruby he'd keep his distance. He intended to keep that promise.

But what other options did he have? Stasi wanted him to guard her friend. The captain had to go along with the royal request. Galen couldn't challenge it—he was already under threat of losing his job. What if he accepted the assignment only to offend Ruby by his closeness? If she complained, Galen would receive the third strike against his record and be kicked off the royal guard.

But if he wasn't there to guard her, who would keep Ruby safe?

Ruby met his eyes as they entered the kitchen, passing through the doorway at almost the same moment, her sudden closeness a reminder of those brief moments when they'd huddled together, out of sight of her attacker. She gave him an uncertain look, half fear, half questioning.

Galen felt his heart twist, his mind made up. He'd keep Ruby safe, whatever the cost.

Even if it cost his job.

FIVE

While the captain took a phone call, Galen stepped into the hall and quickly dialed Ruby's number. She answered after the second ring.

"You're late." In spite of the accusing nature of Ruby's words, her tone sounded lighthearted over the phone.

"I'm sorry," he explained quickly, ready to respond the moment Jason Selini finished with his phone call in the office. "My boss called me in to talk about what happened last night. I didn't think it would take this long."

"Do I need to be there?"

Ruby's question surprised him.

"No, it's fine. It's mostly about guard issues." Like the fact that he might lose his job—something he didn't want Ruby to find out, if he could help it. Knowing Ruby's insatiable curiosity, she'd want to know what he'd done to endanger his position. She'd feel terribly guilty if she learned that he was in trouble for rescuing her two nights before, and for going out in the boat two years ago.

Galen quickly adjusted the plans they'd made for that afternoon. "Can you wait at your apartment until I'm done here? It shouldn't be much longer."

"No problem. I have other things I can work on until then."

"Thank you for being flexible." Galen watched through

the interior window to the captain's office as Selini hung up the phone. "I've got to go."

"Okay, see you—"

Unwilling to waste even a few spare seconds, Galen ended the call and stepped back into the captain's office. To his relief, it appeared some of Selini's initial anger had cooled while he'd been on the phone. Galen felt the faintest twinge of hope.

"Where were we?" Selini ran his hands through his gray-flecked hair. "I'm not happy with how this situation has developed, but at this point, it seems we've painted ourselves into a corner. Ruby trusts you. You're as familiar with these events as anyone. So, while I disagree on principle with the princess's decision to move you from sentinel to bodyguard, nonetheless, I'm going to confirm it. She moved Kirk from sentinel to bodyguard, and that turned out quite well."

"Yes."

"Although I won't have this case ending like theirs."

"Sir?"

"Kirk's engagement to the princess." Selini scowled with displeasure. "And now Linus Murati, attached to the duchess. I don't want the royal guard developing a reputation. Don't get romantically involved with this woman. Your position is precarious enough as it is."

"Yes, of course." Galen tried to speak with gusto, to make it sound as though nothing could be further from his mind.

Dismissed, he hurried through headquarters and across the palace lawn to the interior side entrance to Ruby's apartment building. The ancient servants' quarters had been beautifully renovated, modern conveniences enhancing the artful stonework and exposed timbers giving the building a high-end feel. Galen paused just long enough to press his thumb to the touch pad and waited for his print to register, illuminating a green light that indicated he was cleared to enter.

He headed up the stairs toward her door, eager to get on with the plans he and Ruby had made over supper the evening before. Given the possibility that her attacker was after the jewelry designs, Ruby wanted to visit the studio again to secure more of her notes and other materials that might benefit someone intent on knocking off the princess's designs.

As he approached Ruby's door, Galen steeled his determination. Of course he'd meant every word when he'd assured his superior officer that he wouldn't get involved with Ruby. He'd reminded himself of the importance of keeping his distance ever since the enjoyable meal they'd shared in the palace kitchen with the princess and Kirk the evening before. Ruby made him laugh. She was a good friend.

And that was as far as their relationship would go. "Friends," he reminded himself in a whisper just before he buzzed the intercom under her apartment number. "Just friends."

Then Ruby opened the door, a sincere grin replacing the haunted expression she'd worn the night before. Galen felt a giddy smile rise to his lips.

Just friends had never looked so difficult.

Ruby felt her heart heave a sigh of relief at the sight of Galen. His face was starting to heal. She felt bad about his injuries.

More than that, she was relieved that he'd arrived to escort her to Stasi's studio. The more she'd thought about the possibility of someone breaking into the studio, the more she feared she'd left too much information within easy reach of a thief. Papers she still needed could be filed away in locked cabinets. She'd shred anything that was no longer necessary.

The future of Tate Jewelry rested on the success of her royal jewel replicas. If thieves got their hands on that information ahead of time, Ruby didn't know how she'd salvage her family's stores. Everything her parents had worked so hard for all their lives would be lost. How would she earn back their respect then?

"Thanks for helping me today," Ruby said with sincerity as she pulled her apartment door closed behind her.

"No problem."

But Ruby suspected it might be a problem. "You're not in uniform." She'd immediately noticed his green polo shirt and blue jeans. As they trailed through the hall and down the stairs to the door that led out through the back palace wall, she asked, "Are you off duty?"

"Technically I'm supposed to be off today—"

"I can't impose on your personal time." Ruby slipped in front of him as he reached for the door handle, as if she could physically block him from heading outside with her. She had enough reservations about spending so much time around him. Certainly she shouldn't infringe on his personal time.

"It's fine." Galen grinned one of his half smiles that was almost a smirk. "Captain Selini didn't have any qualms about calling me in today. He's working on his day off, too. Besides, securing these papers is important, right? I'd never forgive myself if anything happened to them. Or to you." As he spoke, he reached past her for the door handle, his last three words softer than the rest, as though he'd realized at the last second he shouldn't speak them aloud, but by then they were already spoken.

Ruby's heart gave a crazy leap, but her feet froze in place. Too late, she stepped away so he could reach the door. His hand brushed her arm, and she felt an embarrassed flush rise through her. "Oh!" She ought to protest further, but words failed her. She had to focus all her suddenly depleted brainpower on stepping out of the way of the door as he opened it for her.

She ducked around his arms, met his eyes briefly and blushed deeper. "Warm day today." She fanned herself as she stepped outside, hoping he'd attribute her sudden color to the heat of the mid-September weather.

"A beautiful day," Galen observed once he'd pulled the

door securely closed behind them. When making their plans the previous evening, they'd debated whether to walk or take a car. Given the lack of parking, taking a car created more difficulties than it solved, taking them far out of range of the palace and the helpful presence of the nearby royal guard— and also introduced the possibility that Ruby's attacker might lie in wait behind the car, if he decided to show up at all. Since the man had only appeared at dusk before, they could assume Ruby would be safest on foot in the bright light of day.

As they started down the cobbled street toward Stasi's studio, Ruby tried frantically to think of something to say to Galen to break the awkward silence. They'd had no trouble chatting over supper last night, but Kirk and Stasi had been with them then. Kirk had told stories about Galen, of the time he'd helped him change a flat tire, and how Galen had been sent by the old, corrupt head of the guard to intercept Kirk and Stasi as they'd tried to escape from the insurgents following the coup against the monarchy earlier that summer.

Rather than stop them, Galen had told Kirk to give him a black eye. Galen had used the injury as an excuse, claiming Kirk had overpowered him.

Galen had turned red at the story and insisted his actions hardly made him a hero, though Kirk and Stasi both insisted that he'd saved their lives and quite possibly the crown. As far as Ruby was concerned, Galen was a hero.

Given the time they would be spending together, she felt she ought to clarify her statements from the summer before, and apologize for the harsh way her words had come out. But the mere thought of that encounter sent embarrassment through her all the way to her toes. She couldn't bring herself to raise the subject.

To her relief, Galen picked a different topic to discuss.

"I don't know a whole lot about jewelry," he confessed as they walked along the street at a leisurely pace. "The princess's designs must be something special though if these guys are after them."

"Oh, they are." Ruby felt a rush of relief. She could talk about jewelry all day. "Stasi's always been a talented designer. Her pieces were selling extremely well, even before she let her name be attached to them. Now that people know they're designed by a princess, they're even more popular."

"But I don't understand when she says she's designing the royal jewels. I thought all the crown jewels already existed."

"The ancient crown jewels are hidden in a secret vault," Ruby related. "Stasi uses them as inspiration for her own pieces, and since I'm her assistant, I have access to the vault. The way I understand it, every member of the royal family has their own jewels. The reigning king is crowned with the same crown worn by his ancestors, but other members of the royal family have jewels designed for them personally, and each king throughout history has had his own personal jewelry, including a unique signet ring."

"So Princess Stasi's designs don't replace the ones in the secret vault?"

"No, but most of them will probably end up in the vault. It's loaded with jewelry from the Lydian royalty of the past twenty centuries."

Galen let out a low whistle. "Would I love to see that. I've studied the history of the monarchy—royal guards are required to memorize the list of kings and queens, along with the dates of their coronations."

"That must be quite a list. Lydia has a long history."

"It is a long list, but I'm glad we're required to learn it. I think it gives us a better appreciation of what we're guarding. Not just a building. Not just people, but a long legacy of faithful leaders who've given their lives to the glory of God and the welfare of the Lydian people."

Ruby's heart swelled as Galen spoke. She heard the note of awe, the trial-tested devotion he felt toward the land that he loved. It left her at a loss for words. He'd always had that love for his country—a love that reminded her why she and Galen could never be together.

He loved the kingdom of Lydia. She loved the tiny kingdom, too, and found it increasingly difficult to leave at the end of each summer visit, but she didn't belong in Lydia. Her place was back in the United States, running Tate Jewelry at her parents' side. It was her duty. Until she repaid her parents for her betrayal years before, she'd always be bound by her responsibility to the family business.

Ruby tried to focus on that goal. She looked ahead of them toward the corner they'd turn to reach Stasi's studio.

A burly figure hurried across the street, glancing briefly their way before disappearing in the direction of Stasi's studio.

With a gasp, Ruby grabbed Galen's arm.

"What is it?"

"Did you see that guy?"

"The bald man?"

"With the tattoo of the eagle on his arm?"

"Was it an eagle?" Galen increased his pace to match Ruby's as she hurried toward the corner. "I couldn't see the whole thing. His sleeve covered part of it."

"I've seen the whole thing before."

"Wait." Galen pulled her to a stop, standing in front of her and looking into her eyes. "You know that guy? He looked tough."

Ruby nodded as the memories caught up to her. "His name is Luciano...something. He was a security guard at our school." She tried to step past Galen, eager to catch up to Luciano and make sure she'd correctly identified him.

Galen blocked her path, looking unhappy at the idea that Ruby might get any closer to the man ahead of them. "Your school?"

"Back in the US—where Stasi and I studied gemology together. We were roommates, you know." Ruby stepped in the other direction, still focused on catching up to the man. What was he doing in Lydia, so close to Stasi's studio?

"He's from the US?" Galen's voice rose with consternation. "And he's *familiar* to you?"

Ruby caught the emphasis Galen placed on the word *familiar,* and recognized it from when she'd used it the evening before. She stopped trying to sidestep Galen and looked into his dark brown eyes, which snapped with zealous concern. She understood now why he'd barred her way.

"What's he doing in Lydia?" Galen glanced warily behind him in the direction the man had disappeared.

Ruby's mouth had gone dry. "The studio is that way. Do you think we should follow him?"

"Not alone." Galen pulled out his phone, then made a face at the screen.

"What?" Ruby had noticed that, in keeping with his off-duty ensemble, Galen wasn't wearing his earpiece.

"I don't know. Captain Selini…" Galen's knuckles whitened as he gripped the phone, clearly wrestling with a decision.

"Your boss?"

Galen nodded. "He gets upset when things go wrong. If that Luciano guy is the man who attacked you, we should catch him. But if he's not, I could get in big trouble for calling guards away from their posts as we are shorthanded."

"Stasi told me all about that." Ruby understood, and she realized why Galen was hesitant to call. "I can't say for certain that the man crossing the street was Luciano. He could be anyone. Don't call."

"You're sure?"

Ruby took Galen's arm and steered him toward the studio again. "Not until we get a better look at this guy. I don't want you to get in trouble with your boss."

Galen hurried along beside her, but he slowed as they

neared the corner. "We're not going after this guy by ourselves."

"Right. We're just trying to get a better look at him—and
to make sure he's not headed toward Stasi's studio." Ruby
glanced around the corner but hung back since Galen grabbed
her arm, and seemed prepared to pull her away if she went
too far.

There were no people or cars on the street, just limestone
cobbles, pots of fragrant bougainvillea and geraniums, and
storefront signs for various offices. Accountants, lawyers,
dentists...nothing that was open on a Saturday. So where
was the man headed? Even if he wasn't Luciano, the man
didn't look like any dentist or accountant she'd ever seen. So
what was he doing in this neighborhood, and where had he
disappeared to?

"Ruby." Galen's voice sounded low and close to her ear.
"I don't have a good feeling about this. That guy is around
here somewhere. If he has partners, we could be walking
into trouble."

Ruby knew Galen was brave. The black eye he'd earned
defending her, along with the one Kirk had given him three
months before, proved that the royal guard wasn't afraid to
take a hit. Which made the apprehension in his voice that
much more unsettling.

She turned to find he had moved closer to her as they
both bent around the corner of the building, looking down
the street toward Stasi's studio. He rested one hand on her
shoulder, the warmth of his fingers spreading through her
cotton blouse.

"If it's just some innocent guy, and you call in extra guards
for nothing, you'll get in trouble," she reminded him.

"And if it's the same man who attacked you before, and
we get too close and something happens to you, I'll never
forgive myself." Galen's eyes locked on hers.

Ruby couldn't look away. She wanted to apologize for her

harsh words the summer before, to clarify, maybe even try to explain. But the danger around them took precedence, no matter how powerful her feelings.

"I should take you back to the safety of the palace," Galen concluded. "Then I can return alone."

"No." Ruby shook her head hard enough to break eye contact. She peeked down the street. "If he was headed toward Stasi's studio, he's already had enough of a head start. We can't walk away, not when we've gotten this close to him."

"Then I need to call in reinforcements."

"But what if it's nothing? Won't your boss be unhappy?" Ruby caught his eye again and immediately wished she hadn't. He was too close, and his determination to protect her only made her unwanted feelings toward him that much stronger.

"I'll take that risk. I'm not putting you in danger."

SIX

Galen placed a call directly to headquarters. Oliver, the tech specialist who coordinated incoming security data, answered. Galen explained the situation. As he waited for Oliver to dispatch officers, Galen kept his eyes alert, watching for any sign of activity, but the street lay empty, deceptively still.

Oliver explained, "Sam and Paul are on their way. They'll come with a car."

Galen thanked Oliver. He'd have liked to call the Sardis police, but all royal property, including Stasi's studio, fell strictly under royal guard jurisdiction. Galen figured Captain Selini would only be that much more furious with him if he got the local authorities involved, especially when Galen wasn't sure what he was up against. The captain would end up with extra paperwork, and he'd blame Galen for it.

Not to mention that the Sardis police wouldn't understand the situation, unlike the royal guards, who were briefed at the start of each shift. Sam and Paul would at least have some context for what they were getting into.

Galen hurriedly updated Ruby, wishing there was a safer spot for them to wait for the backup guards to arrive. Being off duty, he wasn't even wearing body armor, and they were exposed from every direction on the open street.

"What do we do while we wait?" Ruby looked around anxiously, as though Luciano might jump them at any moment.

Given what she'd experienced the two previous evenings, her
fear was understandable.

"The guards will head directly to Stasi's studio. As I recall, there's a building across the street from the studio with
a colonnade. We could head over there and wait."

"Sounds safer than this spot. Let's go."

They proceeded cautiously. Galen stayed between Ruby
and the street, to forestall any danger as much as possible. To
his relief, they reached the decorative stone columns without
incident. The pillars graced the front of a row of offices, set
out less than one yard from the exterior wall, supporting a
second-story balconet above. The colonnade would provide
them with cover if any violence erupted, as well as allowing
them a vantage point from which to observe Stasi's studio.

Together they ducked behind a large column. Only then
did Galen realize how narrow the space actually was. He hesitated, wondering whether he should step away to the shadow
of the next column, or stay at Ruby's side. He could do his
job just as well from the next column over, and turned to
step toward it.

Ruby grabbed his sleeve. "Where are you going?"

"Just giving you space," he quoted her request from the
summer before.

Pain and panic flashed across Ruby's face. "Stay." She
pressed closer to the pillar behind her, making room for him
to share the shadow with her.

Her pretty lips pursed as she looked up at him, clearly
wanting to say something. Finally she found the words. "I
need to apologize for what I said to you last summer."

Galen's thoughts flew back in time to that moment at the
airport when he'd been alone with Ruby. The princess had
disappeared into the restroom, giving Galen the opportunity
he'd prayed for to share his feelings with Ruby and ask her
for a goodbye kiss. But what he'd intended to be a roman-

tic moment had turned embarrassing when she'd refused the kiss, begging him instead to give her space.

When Ruby struggled to speak further, Galen spoke instead. "I'm the one who should apologize. I was out of line. I tried to make our friendship into something it wasn't."

Ruby only shook her head.

Unsure what she meant, Galen offered, "Or perhaps we weren't even friends, just two people—"

"Don't apologize." Ruby took hold of his shirtsleeve again. "You were sweet, a total gentleman. I shouldn't have reacted the way I did. And you weren't out of line."

Galen studied Ruby's face as she spoke, but then a movement past her shoulder caught his eye. "There's a man in the studio." He pointed to a small side office clearly visible through the second-story windows. "Next to the file cabinets."

Her mouth open to speak, Ruby instead turned to look where he pointed. "Is it the same man who attacked me? Is it Luciano?"

"It's not the same guy. He has dark hair—the man you saw was bald."

"He's too far away to tell if that's really hair making his head look dark. Maybe he's wearing a hat. Maybe it's a mask, ready for him to pull down over his eyes."

It was a good point, and yet, "I don't think his shirt looks the same."

"So it's the accomplice?" Ruby's words were nearly drowned out by the sound of a vehicle approaching with a rumble of tires on cobbles.

Galen recognized the royal guard car as it came around the corner.

"He saw them!" Ruby gasped.

She was right. The man in the office above darted for the door. He was going to get away.

Galen stepped into the street and flagged down Sam and Paul. "He was on the second floor, but he heard you coming. There's a rear exit and one out front." Galen pointed as the two men climbed from the car and split up, each headed toward an exit.

To Galen's relief, they'd left the car running. He motioned to Ruby. "Get in the backseat and keep your head down."

"Where are we going?" she asked him as she scrambled through the open door. "Not to the palace?"

Though it would be the safest place for her, Galen knew he only had one shot at catching the intruder, and if he took the time to drive Ruby home, he'd miss it.

"We're going after whoever comes out of that building."

As he spoke, Paul shouted from the far exit.

Galen slid into the driver's seat and put the car in Reverse. It was pointed in the exact opposite direction—no doubt the man in the window had realized that, and headed for the far-thest exit. The street was far too narrow for Galen to turn the car around.

Punching the gas, Galen tore backward, keeping the wheel straight to avoid scraping against the nearby buildings.

Paul darted into the street.

Galen slammed on the brake, narrowly avoiding hitting his fellow guard.

"What's going—"

"Head down!" Galen reminded Ruby as she tried to see what was happening. As soon as Paul leaped out of the way, Galen hit the gas again, backing as far as the next intersection, then whipping the wheel in a tight curve so that the nose of the compact coupe was pointed in the direction Paul had run.

With squealing tires a vehicle took off from the cross-street ahead, leaving the pavement for an instant as it jumped the natural ridge of the centuries-old street.

Galen accelerated after the car, passing Paul just as the guard whipped around, running in the opposite direction. "Ruby, look back and see what Paul's doing," Galen re-quested, wishing he had worn his earpiece so he could hear what his peers were up to—assuming their communication devices hadn't been jammed again.

He kept the car in sight as it made for the busy shopping district directly ahead. No doubt the vehicle had been strategically positioned to reach traffic quickly.

"He's running after a man on foot," Ruby explained. "They went around the corner. I can't see them anymore."

"Another man on foot?" Galen didn't like the sound of it. How many men were they up against? Had the driver ahead of him picked up a third man, or was he only acting as a decoy to draw Galen away?

They entered the shopping district. Startled pedestrians scrambled in front of him, their shopping bags swinging wildly, obstructing his view as cars and bicycles honked at the vehicle he was trying to follow.

Another car pulled out in front of him, then stopped in the middle of the street because pedestrians scrambled to pick up the bags they'd dropped in all the confusion. Pedestrians in Lydia had long enjoyed right of way privileges over vehicles—a freedom Galen had never begrudged them until that moment.

Galen tried to see past the car, but it blocked his view of the street ahead. He opened his door, unbuckled his seat belt and stood, second-guessing his decision to tell Oliver to send the officers stealthily. They'd arrived in a vehicle that wasn't equipped with lights or sirens, leaving him with no way to force the pedestrians to clear the street.

Far ahead he could still see the escaping car.

In front of him, the last woman finished gathering her things and the road-blocking vehicle began to move. Galen slumped back into his seat and got the car in gear, but by the time the car ahead had moved, there was no sign of the vehicle he'd been tailing.

"Are you going to go?" Ruby asked.

"Which way?" Galen's fingers twitched with coursing

adrenaline. He wanted to tear off up the street, but he didn't know which road to take, and there were too many innocent bystanders ahead, blocking his way, risking potential injury if Galen tried to steer the car through their midst.

"I don't know." Ruby's voice caught, and Galen realized the fear and disappointment of the chase, on top of the emotional confession they'd interrupted, were taking their toll on her.

"I'm going to head back and see what Paul found." He carefully turned the car around, grateful the street was wider in the shopping district.

But as he approached the studio, he recognized Paul and Sam walking back to the building from the opposite direction.

"They didn't catch him." Ruby had her head up again, watching through the front windshield and could see the men were alone.

Galen drove up to them and rolled down the window.

"He had a motorcycle waiting down the street." Sam shook his head with regret. "We tried to keep up." He shrugged, the chase obviously futile, man against machine.

"How many men were there?" Galen asked.

"Two came out the front door." Paul pointed to the end of the building he'd covered. "One got in a car, the other on the bike."

"A car?" Galen almost didn't want to know the answer. "Did it have a driver waiting?"

"Yes." Paul answered without hesitation. "He had the motor running and pulled up to meet him. Based on the timing, I'd say they were coordinating their movements, probably through earpieces like ours."

"Did they jam your signal again?"

"Not this time. They must not have been expecting us."

"But," Sam added, "if they're able to jam our signals, wouldn't they be able to listen in on our conversations, as well?"

"You're right." Paul hung his head.

Galen felt the weight of Sam's realization. If their adversaries had been listening to Sam and Paul's conversation, they'd have known the men were after them, and they could listen in on everything the guards might say in the future.

But how were the guards supposed to communicate otherwise? Even if Simon managed to dig up earpieces that worked in some other format, that their opponents couldn't jam or listen in on, it would take time to have them delivered to Lydia, and more time for the guards to acclimate to using them effectively.

Captain Selini wasn't going to like what they'd learned.

More than that, Galen feared the captain wouldn't like what they hadn't learned, either…such as the identity of the intruders and what their determined adversaries were after.

"I'm going to take Ruby to the palace. Do you two want a ride?"

Sam and Paul looked at each other.

"I think we should walk through the building again."

Galen nodded. "Be careful not to touch anything. We'll have to get our investigation crew in there to scour for clues."

"If these guys are half the professionals they seem to be, I doubt the investigators will find anything," Paul predicted.

Ruby let out a tiny groan of disappointment from the backseat, reminding Galen that she could hear everything they said. He was concerned enough about her reaction to what had happened. He didn't need Paul or Sam bolstering her fears.

"Stay safe," Galen called out to the men as they turned back toward the studio. Then he backed down the street, whipped the car around and headed the few blocks toward the palace.

"I never got to secure my papers," Ruby whispered from the backseat, her words so faint she might have only been speaking to herself.

Still, Galen felt he needed to respond to try to reassure her. But what could he say? Everything they'd learned only made the situation worse. The work she loved had been compromised. He couldn't think of one thing they'd gained through their efforts.

"I'm sorry," he told her as he pulled up to the vehicle gate at the palace. "Things can only get better now."

"Can they?"

Galen could hear the discouragement in her voice. As soon as they were out of the car, he'd take a moment to talk to her. He wanted to insist that they'd hit bottom, to convince her there was nowhere else for them to go but up. But as the gate in front of him opened and he pulled through toward the garages, Galen saw a straight-backed figure approaching from the direction of the royal guard headquarters. There was no mistaking the captain's uniform.

Jason Selini did not look happy.

SEVEN

"Oliver dispatched Paul and Sam to Princess Anastasia's studio." Captain Jason Selini scowled at Galen as he stepped out of the car. "I understand there were three men involved in a break-in on royal property, yet none of them were brought into custody."

Ruby clambered out from the backseat, grateful Galen offered her a hand as she stepped onto solid ground. She blinked in the bright sunlight, observing Galen's superior officer as he raked his hands through his hair.

The captain looked upset. Ruby hoped he didn't blame Galen for letting the men get away. Galen still had hold of her hand, and she held on, grateful for the courage his touch imparted.

"Harris." The captain addressed Galen by his last name. "I want to see you in my office immediately. Alone," he added, then glanced at Ruby before turning his back to them both and heading for the royal guard headquarters.

Ruby understood. She wasn't welcome at their meeting. Though she'd have liked to hear what the captain had to say, she needed to find Stasi.

"Are you going to be okay?" Galen asked her softly, meeting her eyes for a long moment in spite of his captain's *immediate* request. She wanted to finish the conversation she'd started, but that would obviously have to wait.

"I need to tell Stasi what happened at the studio. She should be inside the palace having a dance lesson right now. How much can I tell her?"

"As much as you think she's ready to hear. Just make sure she understands that the investigators will need to finish their work before she can go inside. We don't want to risk contamination—"

"Harris!" The captain shouted from the doorway of the guardhouse.

Galen gave her hand a final squeeze as he turned and trotted away.

Ruby watched him go and prayed silently that his superior officer wouldn't take out his obvious anger on Galen. When the guard's lean figure disappeared through the headquarters door, Ruby turned toward the palace. She hated to report more complications to Stasi, who was already under pressure to meet the deadlines that lay ahead. But as first assistant to the princess, Ruby knew she needed to make her report in person.

The marble halls of the palace felt cool, the high ceilings absorbing the heat of the September afternoon. Ruby checked the main ballroom on the first floor, but the room with the pale blue walls, gilt plasterwork and frescoed ceiling sat empty, its heavy chandeliers unlit.

Of course Stasi wasn't having her lesson in the main ballroom. The antique parquet-inlaid floors were spared unnecessary foot traffic so they'd look their best for high celebrations. Quickly, fearing she'd already wasted too much time, and not wanting Stasi to learn of the break-in through the grapevine, Ruby scurried up the stairs to the lesser ballroom.

Music trailed down the airy hallway toward her ears, the sound of laughter rising above the notes. From the sound of it, most of the royal family was present, perfecting their waltzing skills in preparation for the upcoming wedding celebrations, when the eyes of the kingdom and much of the world would be on them.

Breathless from her flight up the long staircase, Ruby paused in the doorway to collect her thoughts. Too much had happened that afternoon, none of it good. What could she tell her friend that wouldn't upset her? Stasi twirled across the floor in Kirk's arms, her skirt swirling, before the movement of the dance turned her toward where Ruby stood.

"Ruby?" The princess nearly stumbled over Kirk's feet. She hurried over to her friend. "What happened? You look terrified."

To Ruby's dismay, the rest of the royals stopped dancing, as well. All eyes turned to her. No doubt they'd all heard about the previous incidents and were anxious to hear the latest development.

Ruby gulped a breath. Reporting to the whole royal family was far more intimidating than sharing the news with her friend. Galen had stressed that no one was to go to the studio, but Ruby couldn't imagine telling Prince Alexander or King Thaddeus that they couldn't do something if they made up their minds to do it. She tried to think how best to start.

"Did someone come after you again?" Stasi asked.

"No." She heard her voice catch as the memory welled up. "They were in the studio."

"Who?" Stasi asked over the collective gasp of her siblings.

"Some big men."

"The same men who attacked you?"

Ruby nodded, and the royals began talking over one another in their haste to learn the details.

"Quiet now." King Thaddeus didn't raise his voice, but his position of authority as the eldest sibling and highest ranking royal silenced the others instantly. "Let's allow her to tell us what happened from the beginning."

Ruby tried, but when she got as far as seeing the man who

looked like Luciano, the security guard from the gemology
school she and Stasi had attended, the princess cut her off.

"Luciano Salvatore?" Stasi gasped.

"Yes. *That* was his last name."

"You're sure it was him?"

"No, not sure at all. It looked like him—big and tough,
with a shaved head and the same eagle tattoo down his arm."

"Sounds like a match," Levi Grenaldo, Princess Isabelle's
fiancé, said. "Why aren't you sure about it?"

"Well." Ruby tried to think. Why wasn't she sure? The man
had certainly looked like Luciano Salvatore. "What would
he be doing in Lydia?"

"There was always something strange about him." Princess Stasi scowled. "He was so chatty, always asking questions. Friendly, but almost too friendly."

"You thought he was friendly?" Ruby hadn't felt that vibe
from the imposing man. "I was scared of him. He had that
crazy scar on the left side of his face—"

"Did the man you saw today have the scar?" Kirk asked.

Ruby closed her eyes and tried to think. She'd only seen
the man in profile, and just for a moment, but he'd had the
left side of his face toward her, its marred surface catching
the sunlight unevenly, deepening the shadows under the old
wound. "He had a scar."

"Then it's got to be the same man, almost certainly." Levi
had been appointed a member of the royal guard mere days
before the ambush on the royal family. He continued to guard
Isabelle, though his engagement to the princess made him
part of the inner circle of royalty. He turned to Kirk, his fellow guard, who stood beside him. "Let's see if we can't find
a picture of this guy."

"And a record," Kirk added.

"Let Ruby finish her story first," Princess Isabelle said.

Ruby got through the rest in spurts, stopping to clarify
every time the royals had a question. When she admitted

that the intruders had evaded capture, Stasi started past her toward the door.

Kirk grabbed his fiancée's arm. "Where do you think you're going?"

"To my studio."

Ruby took Stasi's other arm. "The investigation team—"

But Stasi wouldn't let her finish. "How are they going to know what's out of place? They won't know if anything is missing. I need to be there. You should come, too."

To Ruby's relief, Levi interjected, "Kirk and I need to find out what we can about this Luciano Salvatore person. Then, with the investigation team's approval, Kirk can escort the two of you to the studio."

Kirk nodded along with his friend's plan. "That will give the team a chance to dust for prints before we get there. Then you can talk to them about what might be missing."

To Ruby's relief, Stasi agreed to the plan. The princess promised to call Ruby as soon as they were ready to leave. Until then, Ruby was going to do some research of her own. Her other gemology school classmates would surely remember the chatty guard. Though New York was several time zones behind the kingdom of Lydia, it would be midmorning there at this hour. Maybe some of her friends would be online. As she headed back outside, she prayed someone over there would know more about Luciano Salvatore.

More than anything, she wanted to know what the man was doing in Lydia.

Galen paced the floor behind Kirk's chair, impatient with the way their search was going. They'd found plenty Luciano Salvatores, most of them upstanding citizens who looked nothing at all like the man he'd glimpsed in Lydia that afternoon. They'd even managed to dig up a few of them with criminal records and links to the mob, but their mug shots and personal information didn't come close to describing the man Galen had seen.

"He's way too old," Galen dismissed the next profile Kirk showed him.

"How do you know he's too old?" Kirk challenged.

Princess Anastasia leaned across the arm of Kirk's chair. "He's too small and too old," she agreed. "Luciano can't be much older than any of us. I remember him talking about having served in the military. I think he joined right out of high school or maybe dropped out to join. He's got to be under forty, maybe even younger than thirty."

Kirk found another search result—this time, a youngster on a ball team roster.

"Not that much younger than thirty," the princess corrected with a tiny laugh.

Galen could hear the effort behind her lighthearted words, could feel the rising tension as they drew near the end of possibilities without finding anything. He prayed they'd get a break soon.

"I found him!" Ruby's voice carried through the open door, her excitement authentic.

Galen spun around as she bounded into the room waving a sheet of notebook paper with hastily scrawled notes.

"Where is he?"

"In Lydia, just as we suspected." Ruby laid the paper flat on the desk where they'd been working, and the four of them huddled around it as she quickly explained what she'd turned up.

"Luciano worked as a security guard at the school in New York where Stasi and I studied gemology. He talked to students all the time—went out of his way to befriend everyone."

"Friendly in a creepy sort of way," Stasi offered.

"Definitely creepy, but since he was always so chatty with

the students, I figured there was a chance some of our peers might still keep in touch with him."

"We only graduated a little over a year ago," Stasi agreed. "The students who were a year behind us would have just seen him in May."

"Precisely." Ruby beamed. "Classes have already started for the fall, but guess who's not there?"

"Luciano Salvatore?"

"No one has seen him since the summer session ended three weeks ago. Not only that, but do you remember when Professor Nickel was replaced midsemester our senior year?"

"Who could forget? There were cops all over campus one day, and then Nickel was gone, but nobody knew where, and all the school would tell us was the name of our new instructor."

"Carlton Verretti says he saw Luciano talking to Professor Nickel less than an hour before the cops showed up the day Nickel disappeared."

"When did you talk to Carlton?"

"Just now—he was online. We chatted. He was extremely helpful, since he just finished his final hours of course work this summer. He also told me that ever since the incident with Nickel, he's been wary of Luciano."

"Wait," Kirk interrupted. "This Carlton Verretti fellow— who is he? Can we trust him?"

Ruby nodded. "I've known him since we were kids. He and his older brother Vince both studied gemology. Their parents own the Verretti chain of jewelry stores. My folks know them. We were all the time bumping into one another at trade shows and jewelry events. Our families were really close."

The slightest strain entered Ruby's voice as she ended her statement. Combined with the twinge of pink that colored her pale cheeks, Galen felt curious about just how close the two families had been. But the question hardly seemed related to the case.

"What else did Carlton tell you?" Galen told himself that, based on Ruby's shared history with the man, they could probably trust Carlton. But at the same time, Galen felt a stab of jealousy that the Verretti brothers had known Ruby for so many years—that they ran in the same circle with her family, and would probably see her at jewelry events long after she was gone from his life. He told himself not to be jealous, but he still felt his hands tightening into fists for no good reason.

Ruby ducked her head closer to the three of them and lowered her voice, "Carlton said he's always wondered if Luciano wasn't connected to Nickel's disappearance. So, when Carlton bumped into Luciano on campus at the end of the summer term, he figured it was his last chance to ask him a few questions.

"And then—" Ruby's voice dropped a conspiratorial octave "—Carlton apologized to me for not trying to get in touch with me or Stasi, but he didn't think we were in any danger and he claimed he didn't want to frighten us."

"Frighten us about what?" Stasi sounded plenty frightened.

"Apparently Luciano told Carlton that he was interested in the Lydian royal jewels."

"How does Luciano know about the royal jewels of Lydia?" Stasi sounded offended.

Kirk patted her hand. "Lydia was in the news quite a bit earlier this summer with the insurgent attacks. I'm sure the royal jewels were mentioned in passing."

"Interested how?" Stasi pressed. "Researching them? Or stealing them?"

Ruby shrugged. "Carlton implied that he gave Luciano the benefit of his doubt, thinking he must just want to know more about them. But once I asked Carlton specifically if he knew where Luciano was these days, he spilled the whole story."

"Did he ask why you wanted to know?" Kirk looked concerned.

"He did, but I didn't think it was wise to tell him anything of what we've been dealing with. All I said was that I thought I'd seen Luciano in Lydia—that's when Carlton told me about their conversation."

Stasi looked angry. "So now Luciano and his fellow thugs are running around Lydia, breaking into my studio and attacking Ruby?"

"I'm not so sure it's Luciano." Galen voiced the theory he'd been considering for the past several minutes.

"What do you mean?" Stasi asked. "Of course it is. Ruby saw him."

"I'm sure the man Ruby saw is the same man who worked as a security guard on your campus, the same guy Carlton spoke with. I'm just not convinced his name is really Luciano Salvatore."

"You think it's an alias?" Ruby didn't sound surprised.

Galen appreciated Ruby's calm demeanor, since the princess was upset enough for all of them. "If this guy has a history—he's linked to the disappearance of your professor, for one thing—and if he's the same man who jammed our radios, I'd say he's a professional who knows what he's doing."

"And if he knows what he's doing," Kirk added, "he's not going to use his real name. I doubt he even entered Lydia with the same alias he used at your school. All we have to go on is his physical description. Do you have a picture of him?"

The princess shook her head, and Ruby looked apologetic. "I asked Carlton—he didn't have one, either."

"So," Galen summarized, "the friendly guy who talked to everyone else about their business, and worked at your school for how long?"

"He started at the beginning of our senior year. If he quit at the end of this summer, he'd have been there two years," Ruby explained.

"Two years." Galen picked back up on his thread of reasoning. "Without ever getting caught by you or your friends' cameras? Sounds like a professional to me." What Galen didn't add, because he didn't want to upset the already-shaken princess, was that he didn't know how they were going to catch the man who already had so many advantages over them.

EIGHT

Ruby stared at the soup in her bowl and tried to force herself to eat. The soup, she knew from a previous visit to Lydia, was delicious. And Stasi had remembered how much she'd liked it and had requested the palace chef prepare it to cheer her up. A rainbow of roasted peppers floated alongside olives and chunks of zucchini and beef in a savory broth. The aroma teased her nose, but Ruby's stomach churned with anxiety.

Kirk had insisted Galen join them for supper since they'd made plans to visit the studio later that evening, as soon as the investigation team called to say they were ready for them. Until then, they hashed out theories while Ruby sipped her soup and wished it wasn't so difficult to swallow.

She felt as though she'd betrayed her friend. Granted, she didn't know why Luciano had singled her out as the best way to get his hands on the royal jewels. But he'd chosen her—gone after her specifically twice in a row. What did he think he would gain from grabbing her? Or was she, as her father had long ago suggested, the kind of person who was easily tricked into giving things away without knowing it?

The memory burned through her, not just her father's accusations, but the downfall of her parents business that had begun five years before. She still didn't understand how her father's business records had been breached, but she understood why Gregory Tate had blamed her. She'd let her friends run loose inside their house. Something in her father's office had been disturbed that weekend, and the business had gone sharply downhill after that. She'd never figured out what had happened, but desperately wanted to earn back her parents' trust.

However, the royal wedding jewelry replicas were more than just her hope for saving Tate Jewelry. Princess Stasi was her friend, inviting Ruby to visit her in Lydia every summer since the end of their freshman year. Not only had the royal family supplied Ruby with room and board, but they'd generously taken care of her every need, from transportation to laundry service. Ruby had asked Stasi how she could ever repay her for her generosity, only to realize she'd hurt Stasi's feelings by asking.

But she still felt indebted. When Stasi had offered her replica rights, Ruby finally realized how she could repay her friend. The profits from Stasi's exclusive line of jewelry went to Princess Isabelle's mission digging deep-water wells in Africa. Both princesses were passionate about the life-saving wells, which provided clean drinking water for families who'd never had ready access to a reliable water source before.

The jewelry replicas were also her plan for thanking her friend, as well. A good chunk of the proceeds from each sale would go directly to Isabelle's mission, blessing families across Africa, and indirectly, expressing Ruby's gratitude to the Lydian royal family for all their generosity toward her over the years.

With the Lydian jewels under attack, all Ruby's plans were in limbo. Would Stasi be able to continue her work? Already the princess had started talking about moving the contents of the studio to rooms inside the palace, where they'd be within the safety of the palace gates, under guard night and day. Stasi wasn't happy about the loss of her independence or the possibility that her family members might see their jewels before she was ready to unveil them, but given that her studio was no longer secure, there didn't seem to be any other option.

Even so, moving everything would take days, and all their projects would be that much more vulnerable during the process.

Kirk's phone rang, and Ruby looked up to find Galen gazing at her with concern. While Kirk stepped out to the hall to take the call, Galen leaned toward Ruby.

"Not hungry?"

"Can't swallow," Ruby admitted, finding the kindness in his eyes far too forgiving in contrast to the guilt she felt. "It's all too awful."

Galen didn't argue. He simply gave a sympathetic smile as he looked into her eyes.

Ruby felt her fears subside ever so slightly—which was silly, because nothing had changed. Nothing except remembering that Galen was with her. A moment later she felt a smile tugging at the corner of her own mouth.

"The soup is delicious," Galen added, returning his attention to his bowl.

Ruby dipped her spoon in and pulled out a perfect spoonful, with chunks of pepper and beef and olives in ideal proportion. Galen was right. The soup was delicious. She ate quickly, and had nearly finished when Kirk returned to the room.

"We're cleared to visit the studio," he announced with caution in his voice. "We need to stay together as a group. Don't touch anything without asking first. Is everyone ready?"

Ruby swallowed the last bite and dabbed her mouth with a napkin, then added her voice to the others'. "Ready."

What Ruby wasn't ready for, she discovered once they arrived at the studio, was the creepy feeling of being inside the studio where everything looked just as it had in all the hours she'd worked there since her arrival in Lydia the month before…and yet, she knew their work had been violated. She'd seen the men through the windows, had watched them flee with the guards chasing them. She knew they'd been inside her work space, going through her things.

And yet, she could see no sign that the intruders had been there. The investigation team had left behind plenty of finger-print dust, evidence aplenty that the professionals had been there, but the intruders had passed through without a trace.

Everything was just as she'd left it, as undisturbed as it looked every morning when she arrived at work. The gems she'd painstakingly counted and sorted still sat in their con-tainers. Why hadn't the intruders taken them? Once inside, a robber would be foolish not to grab the easy loot…unless they were after a much bigger prize.

"How do we know they haven't been here before?" The words overflowed from the fear that welled up inside Ruby.

Stasi looked at her with wide eyes. "I was just thinking the same thing. You can't tell anyone's touched anything, can you?"

"They could have been here every night and we wouldn't know. The alarm didn't go off, nothing's been disturbed in my area." She shivered and leaned closer to Stasi. "What about the artifacts you were working with?"

Crouching low behind her desk, Stasi unlatched the hidden panel that revealed a secret compartment alongside the base of the file drawer. The princess let out a sigh of relief. "Un-touched." She scooped up the various necklaces and brace-lets, wrapping them carefully in velvet before tucking them into her bag. "These are going right back into the vault. I'm not taking any chances."

"What about your research?" Ruby understood Stasi's ef-forts to uncover and imitate the jewelry-making techniques that had been lost over the centuries. With no written record or preserved tradition to guide her, Stasi had been examin-ing the centuries-old jewelry to discern what she could of the long-ago methods.

"I'll have to find a more secure location to carry out my

work." Stasi sighed. "Now I want to look at the files. I know you couldn't see exactly what he was looking at through the windows, but maybe we can narrow down what he was after." She led the way to the office.

As Ruby followed, she felt a familiar vibration from within her purse, and pulled out her phone just as it began to ring. "It's my dad," she told the others.

"Go ahead and answer it," Galen said. "I can tell them which drawer he was in."

Ruby nodded as she answered the call.

"Have you seen the news?" Her father didn't return her hello.

"No."

"They've got it. The whole set. It's all in the press release. Exclusive scoop. International papers. They've got it all."

"What?" Ruby wished her father would calm down and explain what he was talking about, but the despair in his voice said enough. She crossed the room to a computer workstation and switched the machine on, hoping to see for herself the news her father was talking about.

"Isabelle's jewels. The wedding is one week from today, and someone has released the whole set. They've scooped our scoop."

"Who released it? How did they know?" Ruby couldn't believe it. Other than the design specifications she'd passed on to her father, which he had forwarded under the utmost secrecy to their production team, no one outside of Stasi's studio was supposed to have that information.

"It's all anonymous. They ship directly from the manufacturer, and I've contacted them already, but they won't say who's behind it. But it doesn't matter. We've lost whatever advantage we had. By the time our replicas are unveiled after the wedding, everyone else will have knocked off the knockoffs, with cheaper imitations, too. They'll undercut us. We'll have to take a loss."

"No!" Ruby had the web browser open now, and had found the story simply by searching *Isabelle Lydian wedding jewelry*. Slowly the truth sunk in. "Don't take a loss."

"What is it?" Stasi came running out of the office. "No!" She echoed when she saw the screen. "My designs were stolen?"

Ruby could only nod while her father continued to predict dire results.

Stasi leaned closer to the screen. "A spring ring clasp? What are we, a dollar store? They got the pendant right, but this is a cheap knockoff."

Though her friend looked insulted, Ruby felt relieved by the discrepancy. Tate Jewelry's replicas had retained the hidden clasp with safety latch integral to the original design. Though it meant the pieces cost more to produce, it also made them higher quality—a distinct advantage over the jewelry she saw on the screen. She tried to convince her father of that fact.

"The Tate Jewelry pieces are much higher quality," she assured her father.

"It won't matter! These are available to order today. No one will need to order ours if they've already bought the cheap ones."

Stasi's eyes widened. Ruby's father's words, shouted in anger, were easy enough for her friend to hear as they echoed through the studio.

"Are the Tate Jewelry replicas ready to sell?" The princess asked.

Ruby repeated the question to her father, though she was nearly certain of the answer.

"They've already shipped to the stores," Gregory Tate's voice carried clearly from the phone. "The web pages are ready to go live with the click of a button. Everything is in place for the release."

"Go live." Stasi said, anger undercutting her voice.

Ruby's jaw dropped.

Galen spoke softly from beside her. "Don't you need Isabelle's permission?"

Stasi pulled out her phone. "I'll call her, but I'm almost certain she'll agree with me on this one. We're not going to allow someone who stole my designs to have a full week's monopoly on the market." A moment later she had her sister on the phone and explained the situation to the elder Lydian princess.

Ruby quickly clarified with her father that he could unveil the higher-quality replicas at a moment's notice.

"I'll emphasize that they're a more accurate reproduction authorized by the royal family," her father assured her.

Princess Stasi turned to Ruby a moment later, a measured smile on her lips. "Isabelle has given her blessing. Go live."

"Go live, Dad," Ruby repeated, a prayer rising up inside her that somehow, in spite of this unexpected setback, the quality of their work would set them above the rest. Otherwise, if her parents had to eat the production costs, they'd end up further behind than before.

They couldn't let that happen. Ruby felt Galen's comforting hand settle on her shoulder as she added, "You have the royal blessing." She hoped it would somehow be enough.

Galen arrived early at the Sardis Cathedral and slipped into a pew near the middle of the sanctuary, where light from the rising sun spilled through the centuries-old stained glass windows, casting brilliantly colored light across the polished oak in front of him. He gripped the seatback as he prayed silently, just as countless other believers had over the years, and watched the colored lights splash across his hands.

So beautiful. So similar to the jewelry Ruby and the princess created, and just as ephemeral. Already the first set of wedding designs had slipped through their fingers, stolen in secret by mysterious intruders they could hardly identify, let alone catch. Galen breathed out his disappointment with heavy exhales, trusting God to understand the burden he carried, even if he couldn't find words to express his feelings of failure and frustration.

Head bowed, eyes closed, lost in prayer, Galen paid no attention to the other people who filtered in around him, taking their places and preparing for the worship service to begin. It wasn't until the choir began to sing the opening notes of their prelude that Galen lifted his eyes and looked around. Far ahead of him, through the crowd, he spotted Ruby's red hair.

She was here. His shift wasn't set to begin until late that afternoon. Ruby sat just behind the royal family, next to Ethan, the royal guard who'd been assigned to her for the morning shift. She was safe.

But once the service ended, the congregants trickled out of their pews, chatting and milling about as they made their way slowly to the large hall where refreshments were served.

Galen lost sight of Ruby. He told himself not to be concerned. There were plenty of guards in the cathedral—both on and off duty. And all the royal guards had been briefed on the situation with Ruby. They'd know to be extra alert.

Still, when he reached the side aisle, Galen used the pedestal riser of an ancient column to gain a foot up so he could peer above the heads of the crowd.

No sign of Ruby, but the royal family had left the sanctuary, as well. Their pews were nearest the wide doors to the fellowship hall, and tradition held that they mingled among their subjects after worship, emphasizing their accessibility and unity with the people. Most likely Ruby had gone in that direction.

But since he had the vantage point, Galen looked behind him, too. The sanctuary had been quite full, and no one looked particularly eager to leave. Galen scoured the crowd for a glimpse of red hair, but saw mostly dark hair or gray.

And bald. Galen focused on the shiny dome atop a thick neck and broad shoulders.

The man was big.

And on the back of his neck the darkened tip of a tattoo peeked out from under his white shirt collar.

Was Luciano Salvatore—or whoever he really was—in the Sardis Cathedral?

Galen's first thought was to find Ruby and be certain she was safe. She wasn't near the bald man, at least. Too many people filled the sanctuary for Galen to try to get any closer to the man, not that Galen was about to push his way past the elderly congregants that filled the wide gap between him and the shiny head near the rear doors. Whoever the man was, he appeared about to exit.

Galen dropped back to the floor and slipped through the milling throng. Ruby should be safe in the fellowship hall, but he needed to see for himself just to be sure.

King Thaddeus stood half a head taller than most of those who surrounded him. Once Galen caught sight of the king, he spotted Queen Monica at her husband's arm, with Prince Peter between them.

Quickly, Galen located the rest of the royals, their guards hovering nearby. There was Linus with Duchess Julia and Levi with an arm around Isabelle. Stasi stood not far from her sister, chatting with some of the other woman Galen recognized as being on Isabelle's bridesmaid list. Kirk Covington sipped coffee patiently, watching his fiancée from just a few feet away.

Galen still didn't see Ruby, or Ethan, for that matter. He sidled over to Kirk. "Did you see which way Ruby went?"

Kirk tore his eyes from the princess for only a moment. "She was headed that direction." He pointed toward the front of the building. "Ethan was with her."

"Thanks." Galen tried not to feel any concern. He couldn't be certain the man he'd seen from the back was the same man who'd broken into the studio the day before. But the man had been headed toward the foyer that led to the front doors. If Ruby exited the fellowship hall going that same direction, her path would cross that of the man Galen had seen.

Impatiently, Galen waited for the dense crowd to shift so he could make his way toward where Ruby had last been seen. With each passing second his heart rate increased, pounding against his chest, urging him forward. He told himself Ethan would protect her.

Then he spotted Ethan in the front foyer, a quizzical expression on his face as he looked all around, even rose up on tiptoe, clearly looking for someone.

Galen cut through the crowd toward his fellow guard. "Where's Ruby?"

"She was just here. She said something I couldn't quite hear and she pulled on my arm. I thought she was on this side of me. I turned around—"

"She's gone?"

Ethan looked sheepish. "She's gone."

NINE

Ruby darted out the front door after the familiar bald-headed figure. What was Luciano Salvatore doing in the Sardis Cathedral? Attending the worship service? It didn't seem likely.

The sun caught the top of the man's head as he reached the bottom of the steps and headed up the sidewalk.

Ruby reached backward to grab Ethan's arm.

Where was Ethan? She'd told him to follow her. Granted, with her smaller size, she fit more easily through the crowd and had lost hold of the guard's arm a second after she'd taken it, but he ought to be behind her. She wasn't supposed to go anywhere without a guard, and Luciano was getting away, headed up the street in the direction of Stasi's studio.

Ruby needed to follow him, but she also needed a guard.

She looked back inside the foyer, blinking as her eyes adjusted to the dimmer light inside. "Galen!" She grinned when she saw her favorite guard darting toward one of the front doors.

"Ruby." He leaped toward her.

"Can you come with me?" Ruby clutched his sleeve as she looked back in the direction Luciano had gone. His shiny head was just visible as he neared the corner. "I lost Ethan and I don't want Luciano to get away."

"Let's hurry. I don't want to lose him again." Galen pulled out his phone but still kept up with her as she hurried down the wide front steps and along the street after the fast-disappearing man. "I sent Ethan back inside to look for you. He said he didn't know where you'd gone—we split up to find you."

"He was supposed to follow me once I saw Luciano." She pointed out the moving figure, still a long city block ahead of them, and moving quickly.

"I saw him, too. I'm calling Ethan to tell him what's up." Galen punched a button on his phone.

"Stay with me." Ruby still had hold of his sleeve, but slid her hand down his arm and took hold of his hand, afraid he might lag behind during his phone call. She didn't want to lose him just as she'd lost Ethan. The contact with his hand was reassuring, even if it sent an unwelcome thrill through her. She ignored her feelings and focused her attention on the darting dome ahead of them.

Galen trotted beside her as he updated his fellow guard on what they were doing. "Grab a couple guards and catch up to us—but stay off the earpiece radios if at all possible. We already know they accessed our frequency, and I don't want these guys to figure out we're on to them. It looks like we're headed to Princess Anastasia's studio. You know the way?…Good."

Traffic filled both lanes of a cross-street as cars trailed in an antlike line down the hill from the cathedral to the restaurant district. Ruby scanned the cars, waiting for a break so they could cross. Luciano turned the corner far ahead of them. He was out of sight, but Ruby was nearly certain she knew where he was headed.

"Now." Galen squeezed her hand and they darted through a gap in the flow of vehicles. They scurried down the next block, slowing their pace as they reached the corner. "Let's try to stay out of sight."

Ruby nodded. She'd been thinking the same thing. True to the neighborhood, the building on the corner housed offices that were closed for the weekend. Ruby bent low as she shuffled over to the very corner of the building and peeked around. Galen hovered above her, peering in the same direction.

"Do you see him?" Galen asked softly.

"No sign of him anywhere. Do you think he may have gone inside again?" She pulled her head back and blinked up at Galen.

"I hate to think he can slip in and out so easily in spite of the security system."

"It didn't stop him yesterday."

"No, but we're getting the locks changed this afternoon, so it should stop him the next time." As he finished speaking, he peeked around the corner again. "There!"

"Where?" Ruby bent to look.

"Across that street, among the pillars where we hid yesterday."

Ruby looked. Luciano—or whatever his name was—lurked in the shade of the colonnade, his face turned upward toward the windows of Stasi's studio where she and Galen had spotted the intruder the day before. "What's he looking at? Do you think he has men inside again?"

"Could be." Galen pulled back and flattened himself against the building, looking the way they'd come. "I'm calling Ethan. If he approaches from that direction, he might scare Luciano off before we get a chance to find out what he's up to."

Ruby kept an eye on their suspect while Galen spoke with Ethan—who appeared behind them a moment later, accompanied by his brother Adam, who was also a royal guard.

"He hasn't moved," Ruby told Galen as he put away his phone.

Galen explained the situation to the brothers, pointing out the suspect before conferring about their next move.

"I think we need to find out what he's looking at," Ruby

insisted, curiosity and concern burning through her. "Something's holding his attention up there. I hate to think what might be going on. They may be finishing whatever business we interrupted yesterday."

"We're supposed to have a guard inside the building around the clock from now on," Galen reminded them.

"Selini assigned Sam to guard it this morning," Ethan explained. "He should be inside."

Ruby swallowed. She'd met Sam. She'd hate to think what could happen to him if he interrupted a robbery in progress. Obviously Sam hadn't called anything in, or there would be more visible guard activity. Was Sam incapacitated? "I have my key," she reminded them. "We can get inside."

"Should we try calling Sam first?" Adam asked.

The men weighed their options. Galen was against using the earpieces. Ruby understood his reluctance. The devices had betrayed him in the past.

"I've got his cell number," Galen pulled out his phone again. "But if he's in there, moving in on these guys, or watching them, we'll give him away if we ring his phone. And he could very likely have his phone set to chime for incoming texts, so that's out of the question, too." The risk carried through his words—if they gave Sam away, the intruders might kill him.

Ruby glanced around the corner to monitor Luciano. The place where he'd stood was empty. "He's gone," she whispered, just as she spotted him walking down the sidewalk on their side of the street. "He's headed this way." She pulled her head back quickly, hoping the man hadn't already seen her. "Don't look. He should come around this corner in less than a minute," she estimated. It wasn't scientific by any means, but she wasn't about to risk looking again just to check his progress. None of them dared show themselves.

"What do we do?" Ethan asked in a hushed voice.

"Jump him?" Galen raised an eyebrow.

The other two nodded, and Galen pulled Ruby back, away from the corner, depositing her in the relative safety of the nearby doorway. "Stay here," he whispered next to her ear, his cheek brushing her as he turned away, raising feelings of intimacy that made her long for his presence the moment he stepped away. "Don't move."

Ruby flattened herself against the cold limestone, pressing her hands against the flounce of her floral skirt, staying out of sight as much as possible, knowing that anything might happen when they captured Luciano. She prayed the guards would be safe. That Galen would be safe.

She heard pounding footsteps that sounded as though they came from around the corner. Was Luciano running? Had he spotted them? An instant later the guards were running, too, and Ruby peeked past the edge of the doorway in time to see Galen leap onto the much bigger bald man's back.

The man staggered forward, hampered by Galen's weight. Luciano attempted to fling Galen off, but Adam and Ethan caught up to him, grabbing him by either arm as they reached the far sidewalk. Luciano grunted something, but Ruby couldn't make out the words.

Galen dropped from the man's back and swept his hands down Luciano's body, pulling a gun from Luciano's lower back and another from under the cuff of his pants. From what Ruby could hear of the conversation, Galen was doing the Lydian guard version of reading the man his rights. She hung back. She'd have liked to be close enough to hear, but Galen wanted her to stay where he'd put her.

When Galen seemed satisfied that the brothers could hold their captive, he pulled out his phone. After a brief conversation he trotted over to Ruby's side.

"We're bringing him in. I called headquarters. They're coming in two cars—one to take in the suspect, the other to make sure you get back safely."

Ruby appreciated Galen's thoughtfulness. "Has he told us anything?"

"Just that he's innocent." Galen shrugged as he hurried back to where the two guards held Luciano. A moment later the first car appeared. To Ruby's disappointment, Galen rode in the vehicle with the suspect, leaving Ethan behind to accompany her back to the palace.

She slid into the backseat of the second car and told herself she had no right to feel disappointed. They'd caught Luciano. She should feel some measure of relief, but she still would have preferred to have Galen sitting beside her.

"Sam checked in," Ethan informed her as he buckled his seat belt. "He saw our scuffle from the window and called my phone. He said he'd spotted the man outside, but that no one's disturbed the studio since he's been there."

"That's a relief." Ruby felt glad Sam was okay, but she didn't understand the rest. Why had Luciano been looking up at the studio if no one was inside? What was he doing in the area, anyway, and why had he been at the cathedral? Too many questions swarmed through her thoughts. "Are we going to question Luciano right away?"

"We?" Ethan laughed. "I'm sure he'll be questioned as soon as possible, but you're not going to be part of it."

They finished the short drive to the palace as the guard spoke. Ruby didn't argue with him. It wasn't his decision to make whether she was there or not, but she felt strongly that, given her role in the events thus far, she ought to be present as he was questioned. The guards wouldn't know anything about the jewelry. They weren't the ones who'd been attacked, and they didn't know the details of Luciano's time as a security guard at her school, or any of the finer subtleties of her conversation with Carlton Verretti. She needed to be there.

Somehow, she'd have to make the guards understand that.

* * *

"You've got the wrong man."

Luciano Salvatore's words echoed through Galen's thoughts as he typed quickly, prepping interrogation notes for Jason Selini as he waited for the captain to arrive at headquarters.

The suspect was bluffing. Had to be. Still, Galen agreed with the same innocent-until-proven-guilty policy the American had voiced as they'd brought him in. Now his stomach churned with doubts. Too many things felt wrong, like why Luciano had been hanging about the studio without going inside, and why they'd captured him so easily. Why would the guilty party return to the scene of the crime, just to circle the building and get himself caught?

Galen would have liked to ask the man himself, but when he'd called his superior officer to let him know they'd apprehended the suspect, Selini had insisted on interrogating the man personally. The captain wouldn't even let Galen in the same room. He'd offered to let Galen watch the conversation from through the one-way glass.

Knowing it would be the best offer he'd get, Galen had thanked the captain and asked if he could submit questions.

To his relief, Captain Selini had seemed reluctantly pleased.

It might be a step in the right direction. Unless Luciano was right and they had the wrong man.

After silently handing his questions to the captain, Galen stepped outside. He'd silenced his phone several times since the church service and didn't want it distracting him again during Salvatore's questioning. He checked the log of missed calls. As he might have guessed, his brothers had been wondering where he was.

Knowing he'd have a few moments while the captain prepared for the interrogation, Galen chose to call Adrian, the youngest of his three older brothers. He had hardly dialed Adrian's number when he saw Ruby approaching from across the terraced lawn. He caught sight of her red hair as it bobbed from behind the bushes, drawing closer, until she bounded out, her flared skirt bouncing as she hurried toward him. He drank in the sight of her—the orange-red poppies on her skirt the exact color of her hair, the green blouse that matched the poppy leaves bringing out the green in her jade eyes.

His heart rate rose with awareness of her presence, but as always, he reminded himself that he had no right to feel what he felt for her. She was his to protect, but never to hold. Whatever she'd been trying to tell him during her apology the day before, she'd never finished speaking, and he wouldn't torture himself with the possibility that she might soften her earlier request for space.

He nodded at her as she approached. She saw his phone and waved silently, hovering some feet away to allow him privacy.

"You missed church." Adrian's voice pulled him back to the purpose of his call.

"I went to the cathedral."

"Mom made dinner."

Galen's stomach growled at the reminder. He hadn't had anything since breakfast. "I got caught up with work."

"I was wondering about that." Adrian wasted no time before asking questions. "What's up with the guard? It's all over the news that Princess Isabelle's jewelry got stolen or something."

"Not the jewels themselves." Galen didn't even know where those were being kept, but he was nearly certain he'd have heard if they were missing. "Just the designs."

"Aren't you supposed to be guarding those things? I thought you said the royal guard was going to be better than ever, now that the insurgents were rooted out."

Galen rubbed his face and tried to think. He'd never measured up to his brothers. The royal guard, in his brothers' eyes, would never be as good as the army. Someday, he'd show them he was every bit as strong and capable as they were, that he'd made the right choice when he'd joined the royal guard instead of staying in the military like the rest of the men in his family. "Princess Isabelle authorized the Tate Jewelry reproductions." Galen stated the facts. "They were bound to be knocked off eventually."

"Before the wedding?"

Galen needed to get off the phone. The interrogation would be starting any minute, if it hadn't already, and by the way Ruby hovered patiently, he guessed she wanted to speak with him first. "I've got work to do. Tell Mom I'm sorry I missed lunch." Galen ended the call before his brother could continue pressing for answers.

Ruby beamed up at him as he put his phone away and stepped toward her.

"Have they started questioning Luciano yet?" she asked.

"They're about to."

"I want to question him, too."

"I'm sorry, you can't." Galen sincerely wished he could tell her otherwise. "Captain Selini won't even let me talk to him."

Her face fell. "But I'm the one who—"

"You can watch with me." Galen could guess what her arguments would be, but he didn't have the authority to give in, no matter how valid he thought her request was. He took her hand and pulled her toward the door and forced his voice to stay level as she gave his hand a squeeze. "That's the best I can do. We'd better hurry." Given what he'd learned of Luciano so far, Galen knew he didn't want to miss a single word of what the man would say.

TEN

"Please state your name."

"Rocco Salvatore."

"Rocco," Ruby mouthed to Galen, surprised she'd never heard him use the name before.

Captain Selini must have been equally surprised. "Do you have an alias?"

"I have two middle names. Sometimes I use those instead of my first name."

"Please state your full name."

"Rocco Federico Luciano Salvatore."

Ruby settled into her seat as the captain continued with his questions, taking painfully long to extract any information from the suspect who sat opposite him. From their vantage point in a darkened adjoining room, she and Galen could only see the captain's back, but Adam and Ethan stood on either side of the suspect, whose scarred face, apart from the occasional smirk, was mostly impassive.

"Do you think he's angry?" She whispered her question close to Galen's ear as Salvatore explained in a flat tone that he'd been in Lydia for over a week.

"The captain or the suspect?" Galen whispered back. "I think they're both angry."

Ruby nodded, processing Galen's observation even as Selini quizzed Salvatore. The suspect claimed he'd been at the cathedral for the worship service, the same as everyone else. When asked why he'd headed toward Stasi's studio, he said he had unfinished business there.

Ruby raised an eyebrow at Galen, who returned the look. She held his gaze perhaps a second too long, feeling a kinship stronger than friendship, wishing she'd had time to apologize to him properly.

There wasn't time now. When Selini asked Salvatore the purpose of his visit to the kingdom, Ruby leaned forward, eager to hear his answer.

"I'm a bounty hunter tracking jewel thieves."

Ruby nearly fell out of her chair.

As Ruby sat listening in shocked silence, the captain slowly and methodically extracted the details from the suspect. Salvatore claimed he'd taken the position as a security guard at her school as cover while he was working on a different case, tracking a wanted jewel thief whose identity had been unknown. Once he'd gathered enough evidence for the police to arrest the thief, Salvatore collected his reward and stayed undercover to pursue another lead against an even bigger ring of thieves, the notorious Bulldog Bandits.

The Bulldog Bandits, Salvatore explained, operated in darkness, breaking into museums, private collectors' homes, and jewelry stores during the night, disabling all alarms and getting away with millions of dollars' worth of jewels before anyone ever detected the thieves were there. The only clue they'd left behind, save for their perfect stealth and penchant for antique pieces with historical value, were a few stray bulldog hairs—hence their nickname.

Ruby listened over her pounding pulse. Her first thought when Salvatore claimed to be a bounty hunter was to assume he was lying. But as he continued with his story, she wasn't so sure. She'd heard of the exploits of the Bulldog Bandits— their operation was a genuine concern for the jewelry industry, especially since pieces they'd stolen occasionally surfaced after changing hands several times on the black market. They weren't just getting away with stealing, but with successfully reselling their goods.

And Salvatore's story fit with Professor Nickel's disappearance. Had Nickel been the jewel thief Salvatore claimed to have been initially trailing?

It was possible.

But Carlton had said that Salvatore was interested in the Lydian jewels. Was Luciano Salvatore the real Bulldog Bandit? All his talk about tracking criminals could easily be a cover story. He claimed he'd gone past the studio after the morning worship service to see if the bandits had returned, that he'd been there the night before trailing them and hoped they'd come back to finish their interrupted work.

Was he telling the truth? Even his reason for working at her alma mater was inconclusive. Maybe Nickel had been on to him, and that's why the professor had disappeared.

Questions spinning through her thoughts, Ruby had to make a conscious effort to pay attention as the captain continued his questions, focusing now on Salvatore's activities on the two evenings when Ruby had been targeted. At first, the suspect seemed to be caught off guard by the question, and Selini had to clarify the exact time before Luciano stated that he'd been exercising at the local gym every evening during those times.

When the captain asked for proof, Salvatore insisted that he'd signed in and out each evening, and that the gym had security cameras that would likely contain footage of his activity inside the building.

"He certainly looks like he exercises," Ruby whispered.

"Harris, contact the front desk at the gym." Captain Selini's voice buzzed through the intercom. "I want scans of Rocco Salvatore's signature with the times he signed in and out, as well as any security footage they can find of him that proves he stayed at the gym between signatures."

Ruby stayed to listen to the rest of the interrogation while Galen left to track down the requested information. In his absence she felt acutely alone. Faint but familiar, his lingering scent reminded her of the hours they'd spent on an island two summers before, lying on the white sand beach, watching falling stars streak across the sky. It was one of her favorite memories, perhaps the most precious event of her whole life. Galen had shared bits of a sermon he'd heard about God creating the stars, and how it had meant God loved each person.

Ruby couldn't remember the specifics, but she'd never forget how very loved she'd felt at that moment. Loved by God, as she'd never felt before.

The memory stirred inside her, along with regret that her apology earlier had been interrupted before she'd had time to explain herself. She needed to talk to Galen. If anything, her attempt at an apology had only made things worse.

She promised herself she'd find time to finish the conversation, but, for now, she needed to focus as the captain continued with the interrogation.

Rocco kept his responses guarded. As far as Ruby could tell, the man wasn't about to admit to the slightest infraction, nor would he tell them anything about the identity of the Bulldog Bandits.

"I've put almost two years into gathering evidence against these guys. All I need is to keep an eye on them until they return to American soil so I can turn them over to the authorities and collect the three million dollar reward. I don't have to tell you anything. In fact—" Rocco Salvatore leaned back in his chair and stretched his massive arms outward in a yawn "—I don't think you have any grounds for keeping me here."

"We need to see if your alibi checks out." Captain Selini turned to Galen, who'd stepped into the room.

"His alibi checks out."

"What about the witness?"

"The witness?"

"The victim? Can she pick him out of a lineup?"

"I'll ask her."

Galen was at her door an instant later.

Ruby was ready with her answer. "He was wearing a mask." After hearing the man's explanation for his activities, Ruby didn't know what to think. Had Rocco Salvatore attacked her three nights before? She couldn't be sure. And if she wasn't sure, she wasn't about to claim otherwise. Not if it meant imprisoning the wrong man.

Captain Selini entered the tiny room behind Galen. "Tell me that's him."

"I can't."

"If you can't tell me that's him, we have to let him go. If we let him go, he could come after you again."

"But what if he's innocent?"

The captain turned to Galen. "How much of the interrogation did she hear?"

"All of it."

Selini threw his hands into the air as though he might punch something, but instead of striking out, his hands sagged to his hair, sweeping it backward as Ruby had seen him do before. "So you let our smooth-talking suspect convince the witness that he didn't do it?"

Ruby realized instantly why the captain was so upset. If she hadn't heard Rocco's explanation, would she have picked him out of a lineup?

Maybe.

And since Galen had let her in to hear Rocco, the captain would blame Galen for letting the suspect go free. She couldn't let Galen get in trouble. She tried to think of some way out. "Let me smell him."

"What?" Galen and the captain asked together.

"The man who attacked me smelled of cigarette smoke."

"Inconclusive. What if he walked through a cloud of smoke

before he grabbed you that night, but he didn't today?" Selini argued.

"He smelled like a smoker. There's a difference. It was coming out his pores. Just let me smell him."

"I can't let the suspect see you," the captain protested.

"What difference does it make? If he's guilty, he already knows who I am. If he's innocent, I have nothing to fear." Ruby thought her reasoning sounded convincing enough.

But Selini shook his head. "There is no legal precedent—"

"Then let him go," Ruby spoke with far more confidence than she felt.

Reluctantly, Selini led her into the next room.

Salvatore sat up straight when he saw Ruby, clearly recognizing her.

She nodded a tacit greeting and approached him cautiously, praying silently that she'd be able to detect enough of a scent to know for sure whether he was the same man. "I'm just going to smell you," she explained as she bent close to his shoulder.

The suspect looked at her warily, but he didn't protest.

Ruby sniffed.

To her surprise, the man didn't smell sweaty, nor did he reek of old smoke or cheap aftershave. In fact, he didn't smell unpleasant at all. "It's faint," she sniffed again. "Is that lavender?"

Rocco's scarred face twisted into a thoughtful expression, then he brightened. "Lavender dryer sheets. I buy the same ones my mom always bought."

Ruby nodded, understanding completely. She still used the same detergents she'd been raised on. It reminded her of home even when she was far away. "It's not him," she announced as she straightened, feeling relieved to be able to say so with assurance.

Captain Selini didn't look at all relieved, but acknowledged, "You're free to go."

* * *

"This way." Galen led Rocco to the exit door. He wanted to ask the man a few questions of his own—questions he hadn't known to put on the list until after he'd heard Rocco's story. "These bandits you're after—what are they doing in Lydia?"

"Plotting to steal the crown jewels."

Galen might have been surprised if he hadn't feared as much already. "When?"

"As soon as they can, I suppose."

"Are you going to try to stop them?" Galen opened the door that led from the royal guard headquarters to the palace grounds. As Rocco stepped through, Ruby came up behind them, following them outside.

Rocco shook his head. "I don't have any sort of jurisdiction in this country. I didn't have the evidence I needed before these guys left the States. Now I've got what I need, but I can't catch them until they're back on American soil."

"Why not?"

Rocco paused as though weighing whether he should take the time to explain. He looked back at Ruby and something in the man's tough exterior softened. "In most U.S. states, a bounty hunter can bring in a wanted fugitive. The law allows for that. In any other country, if I capture someone, I'd be charged with kidnapping, assault—you name it."

Galen grinned. He'd suspected Rocco's plan was something like that, and was glad to have his suspicions confirmed. "If your bandits commit a crime on royal property, or a crime against the crown, the royal guards can arrest them. If you're willing to work with us to keep the crown jewels safe, we'll extradite your bandits to the U.S. and you can claim your reward."

They'd reached the pedestrian gate, which was operated by electronic lock, the controls inside the guardhouse. Rocco Salvatore looked at the gate expectantly.

Galen tried again. "Can you at least tell us the names of the Bulldog Bandits?"

Rocco looked offended, even angry. "I've worked two years on this case. It's my work, my reward. I don't owe you any favors. You still have the guns you took from me."

The man had been carrying the weapons legally, so Galen had no grounds for holding them any longer. Galen pulled the weapons from the back of his waistband, where he'd tucked them out of sight under the lightweight blazer he'd worn to worship that morning. He nodded to the guard in the gatehouse to unlock the gate.

Rocco stepped through.

"Stay inside," Galen told Ruby softly as he stepped out after the man. Once the gate had shut securely behind him, he handed Rocco his weapons, along with a business card that carried his personal cell phone number and that of the main royal guard switchboard. "Think about my offer."

To his relief, Rocco nodded. "I will." He checked his weapons, tucked them back into their holsters, and walked away.

Back inside, Galen looked at Ruby in silence, his thoughts still processing all that Rocco had said. Was the man telling the truth? Would he be willing to work with them?

Ruby must have been pondering similar questions. "Give him time," she said softly.

Galen raised a questioning eyebrow.

"He's upset right now about being interrogated," she explained. "Once he has time to think about your offer, he'll come around, even if it's just for the sake of getting his reward money sooner."

"I hope so." Galen hesitated to voice the rest of his thoughts.

"You're worried that we let the wrong guy go free?" Ruby guessed as they made their way slowly back toward the guardhouse.

"We know the man who attacked you had accomplices. We just don't know who or how many."

"You think Rocco could be one of the Bulldog Bandits, even though he doesn't smell like a smoker?"

Galen tried to process aloud the jumbled thoughts that didn't make sense. "Your friend Carlton told you that Luciano—aka Rocco Salvatore—was after the Lydian royal jewels. We've seen him hanging around Princess Stasi's studio, and now Princess Isabelle's wedding jewelry designs have been scooped."

Ruby stopped in her tracks before they reached the guard building. "The Bulldog Bandits don't care about wedding jewelry designs. They don't do reproductions." She crossed her arms over her chest and met his eyes as she wrestled visibly with the conflicting information. "The Bulldog Bandits have pulled off at least fifteen jewelry heists in the past six years, and every single one of those jobs was made up entirely of jewelry at least a hundred years old, some of it centuries old."

"Maybe they're branching out?"

"They've left behind modern pieces that were in the same case with the jewels they stole. I've read about these guys and the theories of their modus operandi. They clearly cater to a specific clientele and they're not going to risk getting tracked down by lifting jewelry that's not already spoken for."

"Clientele." Galen latched on to the word.

"Collectors—wealthy and unscrupulous, probably drug dealers, pirates or despots—people who've made their money by breaking the law and prefer to spend their money buying things that flaunt their ability to break the law." Ruby made a sour face. "Honest people don't go out of their way to buy stolen property."

Impressed by her knowledge of the underbelly of the jewelry industry, Galen nonetheless wished he knew what to make of all the conflicting clues they'd picked up. He had urgent business to attend to, as well—including following up with Captain Selini, and changing into his guard uniform, since his shift had started half an hour before. "I'm scheduled to guard you this evening," he reminded Ruby. "I need to check in—"

"Of course." Ruby nodded, the vulnerability in her eyes bordering on longing. "And I want to talk to Stasi. She asked to have the files brought to her suite in the palace so she could inspect them thoroughly to see if anything was missing or out of place. Can you look for me at her suite when you're done checking in?"

Galen agreed, but warned her. "I'm sure Captain Selini will want to discuss the interrogation, so I don't know how long I'll be. Just don't leave the palace complex without me."

"I'm not going anywhere without you." Ruby reached for him, resting her small hand on his arm. "I want to finish that conversation we started earlier."

Warmth spread from her fingers through his arm, straight to his heart, carrying hope he wasn't sure he should trust. He wished he could take the time to talk to Ruby that very moment, but the captain was waiting, and Galen couldn't afford to let him grow impatient. He nodded his understanding and Ruby turned away. For a few seconds Galen indulged his eyes, watching her graceful figure retreat.

Then he turned toward headquarters to face the captain.

ELEVEN

To Galen's relief, the captain was too concerned about the fast-approaching royal wedding to spend much time picking apart what they had or hadn't learned from Rocco.

"I don't like the idea that these Bulldog Bandits might be somewhere in Lydia, but we don't have enough information to do anything about them right now and I've got my hands full. Princess Isabelle's wedding coordinator is on her way over here right now to give me my daily lecture—"

"Daily lecture?" Galen repeated, half under his breath. He couldn't imagine anyone reprimanding the imposing captain of the Lydian Royal Guard.

"The woman is a control freak and the current bane of my existence," Jason Selini admitted, his steely defenses lowered enough for Galen to see the weariness behind his eyes. "Just stay on top of this jewelry business and keep me informed of any critical developments. If you can keep Ruby and the royal jewels safe for the next two weeks, you won't have to worry about losing your job."

Galen nodded. "Thank you."

"Dismissed." The captain nodded curtly, the weariness chased from his eyes by sheer determination.

As Galen hurried through the royal gardens toward the palace, he felt a rising well of hope. Maybe he wouldn't lose his job after all. Maybe, if the captain saw that he could capably handle the situation with the royal jewels, he'd be willing to forget all about his transgressions of the past, and his position would be secure. He wouldn't have to be embarrassed to face his brothers after all. He could help restore the royal guard to their former honor.

He traced his way through the back halls to the large front staircase. Bounding to the top of the stairs, Galen was surprised to find the princess, Kirk and Ruby all headed down the hall toward him, their faces pale and drawn.

"What's up?"

"I should have realized it sooner," Princess Stasi answered.

"We were looking at the files," Ruby talked over her friend, "and talking about what we learned from Rocco and Carlton."

"The royal jewels," Kirk explained. "Not the ones Stasi's designing."

Galen had some difficulty following the jumble of words, especially given their ominous tone. "Not the royal wedding jewels?" he clarified.

"The ancient crown jewels of Lydia." Ruby met his eyes.

"The Bulldog Bandits," Kirk added.

"My files contained specifics on the crown jewels." Stasi walked past him toward the stairs. "I was using them as inspiration for my designs, studying their construction and trying to stay as true as possible to Lydian royal jewel traditions. If the bandits are after jewelry with historic value, they were probably trying to use the information in my files to help them access the underground vault. And Ruby—" the princess stopped and looked back up the stairs impatiently.

"That's why they were after Ruby," Kirk finished his fiancée's thought.

Galen turned to Ruby, still not clear about what the royal couple meant.

Ruby looked up at him with regret pooling behind her lashes. "As Stasi's assistant, I'm the only person outside of the royal guard and the royal family with clearance to get inside the vault."

Galen tried to understand. "Without a guard, you were an easy target. They tried to kidnap you to get them inside the vault?"

Kirk answered hollowly, "That may well have been their plan."

Galen shook his head. "Even kidnapped, you wouldn't let them in."

"Not on purpose." Ruby sounded as though she might cry at any moment. "But once they had the information in Stasi's files, they'd know what questions they'd need to ask me—they might even be able to deduce it themselves. And then the only thing they'd still need—" she held out one trembling hand toward him "—is my handprint."

Galen stood still as his shocked mind processed the revelation. Ruby would never let the bandits into the vault. She was far too loyal to her friend—and far too disgusted by the jewel thieves to help them, no matter what threats they might make against her. But ultimately it didn't matter.

If they kidnapped her, they could incapacitate her and use her handprint without her cooperation. Galen realized with horrified fear that Ruby wouldn't need to be conscious for the security pad to read her print. She wouldn't even need to be alive. In fact, for the purposes of the Bulldog Bandits, it might be easier if she wasn't.

The four of them piled into a sedan to drive to the vault and check on the ancient crown jewels. Ruby slumped into the backseat feeling sick. Her father had been right all along. She was the kind of person who could betray a friend without even realizing it. She'd let down her parents and ruined their jewelry business. Isabelle's wedding jewelry had been revealed a week before her wedding. And now the crown jewels of Lydia were in danger. They might even be gone already.

"When was the last time anyone was in the vault? I accompanied the two of you on Monday." Kirk pulled the car through the palace gates as they opened. "And Ruby was first attacked when? Thursday night?"

"Thursday evening shortly before 8:00 p.m.," Galen clarified. "Then she was followed on Friday evening around the same time."

Ruby wanted to add that Galen had kept her safe on that second evening, but she didn't trust her voice.

"They can't get into the vault without a valid handprint—the full hand, not just the thumb like most of our security devices," Stasi rehearsed. "Is it possible for them to lift a clear print and reproduce it somehow?"

"Highly unlikely," Kirk explained. "The print pads are extremely sensitive. They don't just analyze the individual fingerprints, but the whole hand, the position, pressure, distance between fingers—reproducing that via artificial means would be next to impossible, especially without Ruby's full cooperation. And the print pads are connected to the royal guard computer system. Every time a print registers, the user and time stamp are recorded by the computer."

"The computer records could tell us if anyone tried to get in?" Galen clarified.

"Yes, as long as they use a handprint as the system was designed. If they try to circumvent the system somehow, their activity might not register," Kirk explained, then asked the princess, "How many people have clearance to access the vault?"

"Besides my parents and siblings, the captain of the guard appoints three members of the guard, in addition to himself, for the highest level of security clearance. One of the first things I took care of after we regained the crown in June was to make sure all the former guards who had access were removed from the system, and I helped select the new guards who'd have clearance. Jason, Linus, Levi and you." She smiled at her fiancé. "I had Ruby added for practicality's sake, so I don't have to stop working every time I want to reference a setting. But you haven't gone by yourself since Monday?"

"Not this week."

"There you have it, then." Stasi nodded. "The vault should be secure, but I still want to check everything for myself. And maybe while we're there, we can figure out a plan for increasing the vault security."

"There isn't a regular guard posted?" Galen clarified.

"At the main entrance, yes, but there hasn't been a human guard further down the line, not since the new ultra-secure vault was built after the Second World War. One of the primary security features of the current vault is that it's hidden underground. Only those with security clearance know where to find it. Anything more would risk compromising its location. If anyone tries to get past the initial guard, he can trigger an alarm that rings at the royal guard headquarters."

"What if he was shot before he could set off the alarm?" As Ruby voiced the question aloud, her words slowed, grinding almost to a halt, hoping someone would interrupt to calm her fears.

No one spoke.

Finally Kirk offered, "He'd be found by the next guard when he started his shift."

Ruby hardly found the fact reassuring, especially given the Bulldog Bandits' record. Never in all their fifteen heists had they set off a single alarm.

Which meant they might have infiltrated the royal vault already.

Galen could tell that Ruby was upset, but he didn't know what to do about it. His instinct told him to take her hand, maybe even offer a comforting hug, but given the captain's specific instructions not to get involved with his charge, he figured those gestures were off-limits, regardless of what

Ruby had been trying to tell him. His heart said he'd crossed the line already.

He cared about Ruby more than he should as just a friend. In retrospect he realized he probably shouldn't have let her witness Salvatore's interrogation, but his feelings for her had clouded his judgment. He'd let her in because he wanted to make her happy, not because it was the right thing to do. If he had any shot at retaining his position, he needed to do a better job of keeping his feelings under wraps.

Kirk parked the car in the shadow of the old city wall which had encircled the Lydian capital for hundreds of years. In recent centuries Sardis had outgrown the limestone fortifications with their graceful towers, but the old wall remained, well inside the city limits now, a testimony to the long history of the beautiful city Galen called home.

No one spoke as they climbed from the car. The others seemed to know what they were doing—of course, they'd been there before. Galen tagged along, alert, head down, praying silently that the jewels would still be safely inside, and that their visit wouldn't tip anyone off to the treasure that lay hidden somewhere beneath their feet.

The old city wall, much like the palace wall, was dotted with buildings and shops nestled between its buttresses. But unlike the palace wall, which in most places was no more than a story or two high, the city wall towered several stories above them, its ramparts virtually inaccessible above its sheer stone sides.

They approached from inside the old city. Far on the other side of the thick wall, well out of their sight now, the stones would seem to tower even higher, perched as they were on a cliff overlooking the ancient moat. A clear creek filled the trench. Beyond it, a tree-filled park followed the wall for nearly a mile in either direction, providing hiking and outdoor recreation opportunities to the residents and visitors of Sardis.

Kirk led them to what looked like a narrow alleyway between buildings, a booth at the entrance marked Information. The shadow of a man filled the window. Kirk motioned for the rest of them to stay back as he approached.

The shadow moved. Ruby let out a relieved breath, grateful the man wasn't dead. Kirk exchanged words with the guard, then gestured for them to follow. When they reached a steel door built into the base of the wall, he turned to the princess. "Key?"

Anastasia passed him a slender object. "One of only three in existence," she noted.

Galen kept tabs on the various safety features he'd observed. One was the obscurity of the door. If he hadn't grown up near this neighborhood and recognized the particular shops they'd passed, he might have mistaken the narrow alleyway for any of the dozens of others that tunneled through the old city, most of them leading to private courtyards or gardens, some leading to other streets and alleys. When he was younger, he'd actually stopped at the information booth before to ask for directions through the tangled streets of the city. Everyone knew the men in the booth.

No one realized what they were really there for. They'd always given him perfect directions that led him far away from the clandestine entrance. He'd been none the wiser.

After unlocking the door, Kirk handed the key back to the princess and they proceeded inside. "Pull the door shut securely," Kirk requested.

Galen did so, making sure it was locked behind them.

They stood in darkness for one tense moment before Kirk muttered, "There's the switch," and a series of widely spaced lights illumined the narrow path.

"We're inside the wall?" Galen asked, still keeping tabs. "I thought the interiors of the walls had been filled in for safety reasons."

"Most have," Stasi explained as she followed her fiancé down the narrow passage. "And it serves our purposes if people believe that none of the walls are hollow. If people don't know there's a space inside the wall, they won't come looking for it."

Galen ticked off the fourth security feature. Obscure door, disguised guard, exclusive key, passageway thought to be nonexistent. He couldn't help wondering how the Bulldog Bandits would sort out all the details, especially when they were unlikely to ever get past the first door.

Over the next ten minutes he learned of more security features. Kirk unlocked a second door that led to stairs winding upward.

"I thought the vault was underground." Galen was nearly certain he'd heard the others say as much.

"We have to go up to go down," Kirk explained, leading them to the top of a tower. Once they were high above the city, they paused.

Ruby looked out through a high window and sighed. "The view from up here is amazing."

"It's beautiful," Galen agreed as the late-afternoon sunlight caught Ruby's hair, turning it to orange gold. "Which tower is this?"

"They called it The Last Stronghold," Stasi explained. "The moat is just below here. Centuries ago there was a drawbridge, but it was taken down and the entrance walled over. Legend says this is the tower where King John of Lydia and his brother Luke holed up in their battle against the Illyrians. They rode out at dawn, joined forces with the Emperor Charlemagne and defeated the Illyrian army."

"Or so the legend goes." Kirk smiled at his future wife. "That was over twelve hundred years ago."

Galen appreciated the history, but his greatest concern was the security of their location. "These tower windows are open to the air. Couldn't an intruder circumvent the doors we passed through and climb through these windows instead?"

Kirk laughed. "We're over seventy feet off the ground on

the city side. You'd need a crane to reach this tower, but there's not a street nearby wide enough to park one."

"But the rooftops—"

"None of them are directly beneath us. The closest are still more than fifty feet below—too low to reach the windows with the tallest ladder, even if you had permission from the store owners to climb up on their roof, even if the angles to the windows weren't impossible to navigate from a ladder." Kirk dismissed the possibility.

"What about the other side of the wall?"

"The park is too dense with trees for a crane, and besides, the tower is nearly a hundred feet up from the moat. Perhaps a determined intruder could use a helicopter to reach the windows, but they wouldn't go unnoticed. Even if an experienced rock-wall climber tried to scale the wall itself, the ancient limestone is too porous for suction-securing devices to hold and too crumbly to allow a decent handhold or foothold." Kirk crouched near the floor. "Now watch closely for the hidden staircase."

Galen did as instructed. The stairs they'd taken had wound around the perimeter of the tower, lit by arrow-slit windows at even intervals. Kirk pivoted back a large stone from the cobbled squares that made up the floor. The rock raised a panel, a trapdoor that hid a narrow, far more steeply winding set of stairs.

"The escape hatch," the princess explained. "Centuries ago, if these towers were ever taken, the men defending them had a means of falling back." She slid her fingers along a slender silvery band. "If the guard in the information booth triggers the alarm, this bulletproof panel will slide closed, along with three other panels between here and the vault. They only come open again with a complicated key code, known only to the head of the guard and the king."

Kirk led the way down the ancient stone stairs.

As they made the long twirling trip down, Galen prayed

that they'd find the jewels undisturbed in the vault. They'd seen nothing that might indicate anyone else had passed this way since Ruby had visited with Kirk and the princess on Monday, but given what he understood of the Bulldog Bandits, that was hardly reassuring. Rocco had said the jewel thieves came and went without a trace, save for a few stray bulldog hairs.

At the bottom of the stairs they followed another short hallway, ending in what looked like, in the weak light from the lone bulb far behind them, a blank stone wall. But the princess slipped her hand into a space between the stones and peeled back the false wall easily.

"It's on rollers," she explained. "The track is hidden by the door—you can only see it once you roll it back."

As Galen stepped through after the others, he looked down and saw the narrow rut where the casters traveled.

Then Kirk switched on another light and a wall-size surface like stainless steel gleamed in front of them.

"Titanium alloy," Kirk explained, rapping the silvery sheen with his knuckles. "Seven layers thick. Impervious to gunfire and anything but the most high-powered explosives."

"Any bomb strong enough to put a dent in the vault would most likely destroy everything on the other side, besides bringing down the tower and the streets above us in a giant pile of rubble," the princess added, sliding a much smaller stone veneer panel to the side, revealing a larger version of the thumb pads the palace used as a basic security measure.

Princess Stasi turned to her assistant. "Why don't you show us how it's done, Ruby?"

Ruby nodded silently, her eyes wide as she stepped forward and pressed her hand to the surface. A green outline shimmered on the dark surface and a keypad appeared beneath her hand. "Acts 16:14, 40." Ruby recited the code softly as she punched in the letters and numbers.

Galen recognized the reference—the two Bible verses

about Lydia, the founding mother of the house church that had been the start of the Kingdom of Lydia. No sooner had Ruby entered the code than a green light illuminated numbers above the door, counting down from ten.

"Once the light turns on, you have ten seconds to get through the door before it closes automatically behind you—another security feature. You have to reenter the code from the other side to leave. There's an override button inside to make the door close more quickly, but nothing to keep it open. If it were to stay open longer than ten seconds, it would trigger the alarm at headquarters." Kirk explained as he grasped the knob at the right side of the door, gave it half a turn and pulled the door open.

"Nothing sounds here?" Galen clarified.

"Nothing ever sounds here," the princess confirmed as she stepped into the vault. "If the vault was compromised, we wouldn't want anything to alert the trespassers that guards were on their way."

Galen caught Ruby's eyes for just a moment as they stepped in after the princess. Ruby's tiny, hope-filled smile encouraged him as he braced himself for what they'd see inside, and prayed the crown jewels would be undisturbed.

TWELVE

"Oh, wow." Ruby's voice caught in her throat as she entered the chamber. Emotion filled her, welling up in her throat and her eyes. She blinked it away, swallowing repeatedly and sucking in a steadying breath of the cool air inside the vault, leaning back slightly against Galen's steady frame, grateful he was near.

"I had no idea," Galen whispered, awe in his voice as he gently squeezed her shoulder.

Ruby could only nod in agreement. Though she'd visited the vault several times now, the splendor of the space never failed to move her. Inside the vault a long hallway led forward in time, marching through the centuries past glass cases, each settled in front of statues and portraits of the kings and queens whose jewelry lay on the black velvet surfaces within each case. Often the very necklaces, signet rings, scepters and tiaras pictured in the portraits lay in the cases below, alongside other more varied riches: brooches, pendants, bracelets, letter openers, gold-encased Bibles, jewel-encrusted pencil cases, combs, mirrors, inkstands and pocket watches.

"In the early years of Lydia's history, the jewelry was much simpler, favoring amethysts in reference to the founding mother, Lydia's, work in purple cloth," Stasi explained as she passed slowly down the aisle toward the more modern pieces at the rear of the vault. "Once we reach the era of

Charlemagne, we see the repeated image of the Carolingian cross—four trefoil knots that meet in the middle."

"Nothing's been disturbed?" Kirk asked.

"Not that I can tell." Stasi smiled at her fiancé. "I'd have to examine the pieces more closely to be certain they haven't been replaced with fakes, but the Bulldog Bandits aren't known for bothering with those kinds of details, are they, Ruby?"

"Not that I've ever heard." Ruby felt her tension ease with the reassurance that the crown jewels were, thus far at least, safe. The bandits had a history of taking everything they wanted in one clandestine hit. She'd been trying to recall all she could of the details she'd read and heard of the bandits' activities.

Now she wanted to apply what she knew in hopes of saving the Lydian crown jewels. "The Bulldog Bandits work at night when stores and museums are closed. They override the security systems. No alarm, no matter how high-tech, has ever gone off during any of their heists."

"What about human guards?" Galen asked.

Ruby swallowed. She recalled that detail with chilling certainty. "They kill the guards before they can sound an alarm—usually by shooting them in the back of the head."

"The guards never knew what hit them?"

"They never saw it coming."

"In that case—" Galen crossed his arms over his chest, and Ruby immediately missed his hand on her shoulder. "We have an advantage. We've had some warning when the others didn't."

Ruby appreciated his attitude. "How can we leverage that advantage to save the royal jewels? I'd hate to put a live guard down here, not if the bandits are just going to shoot him. In fact, I think that man in the information booth should be better protected."

"He's behind bulletproof glass," Stasi reassured her. "Even

assuming the bandits got this far, the cases each have a laser-activated security alarm. If the glass is broken or removed, or anything interrupts the beam of the interior lasers, an alarm goes off at the royal guard headquarters."

"But if they have a valid thumbprint and know the code for each case, they can open the cases just like we do and take the contents without triggering anything," Ruby reminded her friend.

"Each case has a unique code?" Galen asked.

"Yes," Stasi explained. "The code is the coronation date of the monarch whose jewels are in each case."

"All the royal guards have the coronation dates memorized," Ruby mused aloud.

"The coronation dates are public knowledge," Stasi admitted, "but the fact that they're the code is a secret known only to those who've been inside the vault. Just like the Bible reference for the main door, they insure that only those who value Lydia's history and heritage can access the jewels."

"But if they're stolen—" Galen began.

"We're not going to let them be stolen," Stasi interrupted him.

"I understand—" Galen nodded patiently "—but if any piece is removed from this vault, do we have a way of tracking it?"

"These are historical artifacts," Stasi reminded him curtly. "They've never been altered in any way."

"If the bandits get their hands on them, alterations will be the least of their crimes," Kirk reminded his fiancée.

Ruby understood how protective Stasi felt about the jewels, but Galen had a valid point, and her friend needed to understand it. "If we planted tracking devices on select pieces, we could find the jewels again, even if our worst fears are realized." She placed a hand on Stasi's arm as she spoke.

Stasi closed her eyes. "I hate to think that's necessary." She shook her head regretfully. "But you're right. They would have to be extremely small devices. I don't believe we have anything like that readily available in Lydia. We'd have to order something."

"I don't want to think that the bandits could get this far." Galen's voice was solemn. "But if they did—" His words trailed off, their warning lingering in the cold air of the vault.

Silently they walked the aisle between the glass cases. Ruby paused several times to look at the kings and queens in the portraits. Despite their gentle faces and compassionate smiles, their eyes held the same determination Ruby had seen in Stasi's eyes so many times—the tenacity to keep their kingdom safe from any and every invader down through the centuries.

It was a legacy Ruby hoped to preserve. But what if her father was right? What if she betrayed her friends unwittingly, just as she'd betrayed her family?

Galen kept a close eye on Ruby as they headed back to the palace. The tension she carried in her shoulders and the balled fists of her hands had eased somewhat once she'd seen that the crown jewels hadn't been disturbed, but anxiety still shadowed her eyes. He waited until Kirk and Stasi went back inside the palace, leaving him alone with Ruby in the back garden as late afternoon gave way to evening. She'd said she wanted to speak with him, but now she seemed lost in her thoughts, overwhelmed by all they'd seen and learned.

He chose his words cautiously, not wanting to upset her further. "I feel reassured after seeing all the security features protecting the crown jewels."

Ruby nodded a little too quickly and blew out a breath, but didn't meet his eyes. They'd wandered slowly toward one of the garden fountains, its water cascading gently down, catching the last of the evening sunlight.

"You're still worried about the jewels?" He didn't know what else to say, but he couldn't stand for her to carry her burden alone. In all the time they'd spent together over the previous summers, Ruby had almost always been carefree and joyful. The change tore at him.

Ruby trailed one hand through the clear water of the fountain. Finally she sat on the stonework edge and looked up at him. "I'm the weak link," she said, her voice so soft Galen had to strain to hear her over the fountain.

He sat beside her. "What do you mean?"

"They came after *me*. They attacked me to get my handprint and any other information they still needed."

"Their only other choices would be guards or royals under guard. You weren't guarded. It's nothing personal. It's an oversight—you should have had a guard from the moment you were given high-level security clearance, but we've been shorthanded." Galen knew Ruby had been surrounded by guards both inside the palace walls and when she was at Stasi's studio. It was only when she had walked home without her friend that she'd been vulnerable.

But Ruby pinched her lips together and shook her head. "It's not that. It's me."

"What do you mean?"

"I hate to tell you. It's so awful."

Concerned now, Galen took her hand. "Please tell me."

Ruby stared at the falling water for several long minutes. Galen waited patiently, praying silently for his friend.

Finally Ruby offered, "My parents own a chain of jewelry stores."

"Tate Jewelry." Galen nodded, aware that her position as heir to the business placed her on a much higher social rung than the one he occupied.

"They expanded several years ago. It was a risky venture, but my parents had realized that if they ever wanted to be able to afford to retire, they needed more than the revenue they were currently making. At first it appeared things were going well." She sighed and stared at the water.

"At first?"

Ruby shook her head. "Everything took a turn for the worse all at one moment. Our suppliers turned on us, the competition undercut our prices with alarming precision, it was as though someone was on the inside, telling everyone else how to ruin us."

"I'm sorry," Galen said when Ruby paused again.

"It was my fault."

"How?"

"I don't know. I can't think what I might have done, but the trouble all began the very week after my high school graduation party. We had over a hundred people at our house. My parents and their friends mostly stayed outside on the back deck and gazebo, but I let my friends come inside the house." Ruby took a shaky breath. "My father is convinced that one of my friends did something—put a bug in his home office or something."

"Did your friends go in his office?"

"They weren't supposed to. It was locked, but my father threw a fit when he unlocked the door the next morning. He claimed his papers were out of order and blamed me for letting my friends in. Then when the business tanked…" She pinched her eyes shut and turned her face toward the sky.

Galen waited, not wanting to hear, wishing Ruby wouldn't have had to experience the things she'd already told him.

She let out a slow breath. "He said it was my fault. He said I had betrayed him."

"But you didn't do anything. You didn't know—"

"I betrayed my family without even knowing it." Ruby stood and turned her back to him, holding out her hand and staring at her palm, as though the print might yet let the bandits reach the jewels. "And without knowing it, I've betrayed my best friend's family, too."

"You haven't betrayed them." Galen stood and linked his fingers through hers. "The jewels are still safe."

"For how much longer? We don't know who these bandits are or where they are or when they might strike." Ruby choked back a sob. "I should leave Lydia."

"No," Galen breathed out the word, wrapping his other arm protectively around Ruby's waist as if he could hold her there forever.

"If I'm not here, they can't use my handprint."

"If you're gone, the princess won't be able to finish her jewelry designs in time for the other weddings."

"That's the other thing." Ruby turned and met his eyes for the first time. "The designs. How do you think those leaked out?"

"It could have been anything."

"It could have been me."

"How?"

"When I forwarded the designs to my father. The bug in his office—"

"You've never gotten rid of it?"

"We've never found it. We're not even sure there is one, but after what's happened, I realize I've been foolish to assume the designs would be safe. For the past five years Tate Jewelry has been floundering, constantly outmaneuvered by her competitors. The replicas of the royal jewels were my plan to save the company."

"Ruby." Galen still had his arm around her waist, and pulled her closer now that she was facing him, encircling her in his arms. "It's not your fault."

"The evidence says otherwise." The tension in her shoulders eased as she let her forehead rest on his shoulder.

He pulled her closer, glad for the tall manicured bushes that encircled the fountain and shielded them from view. Evening was falling, but the garden lights had not yet come on. No one could see them, not even from the high palace windows, thanks to the distance and the lack of light.

Not that Galen would have let her go, even if he'd thought

someone might see them. Ruby was carrying far too much guilt. He felt its heavy weight. She gripped his shoulders, pulling him closer, burying her face in his shoulder as she wrestled with her burden.

"It's not your fault," he whispered, rubbing her back gently, wishing he could chase away all the tension and worry she'd bottled up inside. "You didn't betray anyone."

"I wish I could believe that."

"Believe it. It's true. You're a good friend. The princess raves about what a faithful friend you've always been."

"But if I've betrayed her—"

"You won't. You didn't. Besides, you've always been a good friend to me. Nothing you've done or ever will do could change that."

"That's the other thing." Ruby shook her head. "Last summer when we were at the airport, you asked if you could kiss me goodbye. It was the single most romantic moment of my life and I told you to back off, to give me space."

Galen wasn't certain what she was trying to say. He let go of her and stepped back. "I'm sorry, you're right."

"No." She reached for him. "That's not what I meant. I don't want you to stay away from me."

Torn by uncertainty, Galen met her eyes. "What do you want, Ruby?" He extended his arm, brushing the tips of her fingers with his, unsure whether he was welcome to take her hand.

She took a step closer. "When Stasi finishes her designs, I have to return to America. I love this kingdom. It hurts to leave. And I'm afraid." Slowly she slid her fingers forward until they laced through his. She held his hand securely. "If I let myself give in to my feelings for you, I'm afraid I won't be able to leave."

Galen wanted to tell her how he felt about her, but the captain's warnings pounded through him with every beat of his heart. He couldn't speak, but he couldn't walk away, either.

Ruby's hands slid down his back to his waist, pulled him closer even as she lifted her face. Her hair brushed his cheek. Her nose traced his jawline.

He wanted to kiss her. He'd wanted to kiss her for a long time, but it had never been so difficult for him to resist. As long as he kept his eyes shut and didn't look at her, he should be able to hold out.

"Galen?" Her voice was soft, her mouth so near his ear he felt her breath caress his cheek.

He couldn't keep his eyes closed any longer, but tipped his head and looked into her eyes.

Trust and uncertainty and affection shimmered in their jade-green depths. If he'd wanted his feelings returned, he'd have hoped to see that affection there. But since he couldn't allow himself to get any closer to Ruby, the sight of it chilled him. But in the midst of all the longing in her eyes, he saw that she questioned whether he felt things for her that he wasn't supposed to feel.

The things he'd always felt, but kept buried.

Push her away or keep her close?

He could feel her heartbeat as he held her tight against him, each beat increasing the urgency of his answer. If he pushed her away, she'd feel hurt. She already felt hurt. He couldn't add to that, not when he'd always cared for her, not after she'd shared her deepest fears with him.

To deny the things he felt would be like lying. He couldn't lie to Ruby, of all people.

He bent his head.

She lifted hers.

Her lips were soft, warm, blissful.

The last of the tension she'd been carrying seemed to evaporate under his hands. Perhaps he should have kissed her long before. Perhaps he should never stop.

She rose up on her toes and he nearly lifted her off the ground, wanting to be closer, as though the fervency of his kisses could make up for all the times he hadn't kissed her over the years.

"That friend thing," Ruby whispered breathlessly between kisses. "Does this change that?"

Her eyes sparkled mischievously.

Galen laughed. She'd caught him there. "More than a friend," he whispered, kissing her again.

"Galen." His name echoed from far away. "Galen?" The voice was closer now, not Ruby's voice at all.

"Galen Harris." It was Linus's voice, and Galen lifted his eyes to see his fellow guard appear through the bushes from the direction of guard headquarters. "Phone call—for you. Rocco Salvatore?"

Ruby jumped away from him and Galen dropped his arms. "Why didn't he call me directly?" He found his phone and looked at the screen. "One missed call. Why didn't I hear it ring?"

"I have a theory," Linus volunteered with a smirk, having witnessed enough of the kiss to know why Galen hadn't heard him approaching.

"There's no cell phone service in the vault," Ruby explained. "It's too far underground."

"He's waiting on the main switchboard line." Linus led the way toward headquarters.

Galen hurried after him, mindful that Rocco wouldn't appreciate waiting, not after the way they'd inconvenienced him already. He caught up to Linus as they trotted through the maze of bushes. "Please don't tell the captain what you saw," he requested.

Linus laughed. "I won't."

But as they cleared the last of the bushes, Galen saw Captain Selini waiting for them, his arms crossed, his face perpetually stern. "Don't tell me what?"

THIRTEEN

Ruby hurried to keep up with the guards, unsure whether she could find her way through the garden maze if she lost them. Linus hadn't technically invited her to follow, but she figured whatever Rocco Salvatore had to say was as much her business as anyone else's, and anyway, Galen was supposed to be guarding her. She was supposed to stick with him.

She thought she heard voices up ahead, just before she came around a corner and slammed into Galen's back. "Sorry," she whispered, steadying herself with one hand at his waist, holding on another moment for the reassurance she felt from the contact.

"What isn't he supposed to tell me?" The captain raised an eyebrow, and Ruby realized he seemed to be glaring at the place where her hand still rested at Galen's waist.

She moved her hand, guilty. How would the captain respond if he knew she'd been kissing Galen?

"Harris?" Selini prompted.

But Linus inserted himself in the conversation. "The phone call, Captain. We don't want Rocco to get tired of waiting and change his mind."

"This way." Captain Selini led them inside almost reluctantly. The angry look he flashed them promised that he wasn't going to let the matter drop entirely.

Ruby hurried to keep up, questions swirling. Why had

Rocco called? Was he going to help them? Or was he really guilty, and only calling to feed them misinformation and throw them off his trail?

They stopped in a conference room, and the captain directed Galen to a phone in a small room on the other side of a glass partition. Galen nodded, clearly understanding what to do.

Once Galen picked up the phone and started talking, Ruby understood. A speaker in the middle of the conference table allowed everyone in the room to hear Galen's conversation, but the wall between them prevented Rocco from picking up the noises of the others listening in.

"I thought about your offer. I want to talk with you in person." Rocco's voice was deep, his accent distinctly East Coast American; Ruby had never bothered to sort out precisely where. Not Boston. New Jersey maybe? She couldn't tell.

"I'm sure we can work something out." Galen watched the rest of the guards through the glass, his eyebrows up, questioning, looking for input.

The captain nodded sternly.

Galen's face relaxed. "When would you like to meet?"

"Soon. Tonight, if possible."

"That should be fine. Where would you like to meet?"

"North of the marina. There's a road—Seaview Drive?"

"I know it."

"It follows the coastline. There's a trail on the bluffs overlooking the marina—"

"I know the one."

"Can you be there in an hour?"

Galen raised his eyebrows.

Selini nodded.

"No problem."

"Good. See you in one hour. And bring Ruby."

Galen opened his mouth, but a tiny click cut him off, followed by a dial tone that said Rocco was gone. Shaking his head, Galen rounded the corner and entered the conference room, his eyes darting from the captain to Ruby and back again.

"Bring Ruby?" Captain Selini repeated, raking his hair back. "Why? Why does he need Ruby?"

Galen quickly related the handprint theory they'd worked out that afternoon with Kirk and Stasi.

"So this Rocco Salvatore is one of the Bulldog Bandits?" The captain seethed.

Ruby cleared her throat. "We don't know. He claims he's tracking the bandits—"

"Yeah, he's a bounty hunter. I heard his whole cover story." The captain blew out a furious breath. "Who is he really, and why does he want Galen to bring you out to the bluffs in the middle of the night?"

"I told him we could work with him," Galen explained. "He says he wants to capture the bandits for the reward money. We want to keep the crown jewels safe. If he's really a bounty hunter, this could work out well for both sides."

"And if he's really one of the bandits, what then?"

"I don't think he's a bandit." Ruby had been puzzling over the question in the back of her mind, and she'd realized a few things.

"Because he smells like lavender?" Selini didn't try to disguise the sarcasm in his voice.

"Because he was a security guard at my school for the last two years, at the height of the Bulldog Bandit heists, most of which took place hundreds of miles from our campus, even on other continents. How would he have had time to stake out those jobs and still show up for work each day?"

"When were the heists? When was he at work? Have you cross-checked this?"

"No," Ruby admitted. "But we could find the dates with the news releases—"

The captain snapped his fingers at Linus, who'd been standing by since he'd escorted them in. "Get me those dates."

"Yes, sir." Linus hurried away.

Ruby prayed Linus would find the information quickly. She didn't know how long it would take them to travel to the bluffs above the marina, but they had less than an hour before they needed to be there.

And she got the feeling Rocco wouldn't like it if they were late.

Darkness had fallen by the time they reached the bluffs. Galen felt uneasy. Even the light of the moon and stars were hidden by streams of clouds that chased each other across the sky, casting shadows that moved like men.

Or maybe they were men.

Where were the bandits? How many men did they have, and was Rocco Salvatore one of them?

"We'll park the car off the next spur and walk back this way." Captain Selini reviewed the plan as they approached the trail Rocco had specified. "Don't be afraid to use your earpiece to contact us. We'll have your back."

"Thank you." Galen unbuckled his seat belt as the vehicle slowed to a stop. He had no intention of using the earpieces, not unless he had no other choice. The Bulldog Bandits already had every other advantage over them. Why should they be privy to their every conversation, too?

Ruby climbed from the backseat ahead of him, then waited for him to lead her to the path. Though he'd hiked the bluffs countless times over the years, the darkness transformed the peaceful coastline. As the captain and Linus drove off behind them, Galen paused at the head of the trail to get his bearings.

"What is it?" Ruby looked up at him with uncertainty.

"This way." Galen extended his hand and Ruby took it. If they hadn't been in such a hurry, he might have taken a moment to reassure her, to hold her tight again as he longed to.

As it was, they'd debated whether Ruby would be allowed to come with him up until the moment it was time to leave. Linus had dug up the dates of the Bulldog Bandit heists, but they'd overlapped enough with school holidays and other various unknowns that they couldn't determine whether the evidence they had proved or disproved Rocco's cover. There hadn't been time to dig any deeper.

Was Rocco Salvatore one of the Bulldog Bandits? They simply didn't have enough information to say either way.

Now Galen had to focus on watching and listening, and staying on the trail in the darkness. He'd been against the idea of bringing Ruby along. The risks simply seemed too great. But Ruby stood fiercely by her earlier determination that Rocco wasn't her attacker from the week before, and Captain Selini felt the risk was worth taking if it meant they might learn more about what was going on.

Galen understood. The captain wanted to put the whole issue behind him so the guards could focus on the wedding later in the week. From a purely practical standpoint his position made sense. There would be hundreds of guests in town for Princess Isabelle's wedding to Levi Grenaldo, including media representatives and many prominent families from the region. And the captain had that bully of a wedding planner hounding him at every turn.

Of course the captain wanted to cooperate with Rocco.

"Watch out." Galen took half a step back and held out his arms to prevent Ruby from stepping past him as pattering gravel rained down from above, peppering the trail just ahead of them.

"What's that?" Ruby asked quietly.

Galen strained to see, but between the lip of the cliff above and the thick darkness of the cloudy night sky, he couldn't see anything but blackness and shadows.

Ruby stepped forward. "Is it safe?"

She'd hardly spoken when more gravel fell, this time with larger rocks that clattered loudly down the cliff.

"Stay back." Galen wrapped an arm around her waist and ducked against the wall of the cliff, under the relative safety of the outcropping above. "Shh," he urged her silently when she opened her mouth again.

He listened carefully. The rocks had stopped falling, but that didn't mean the trail was safe. Something had dislodged the gravel above them. Galen was familiar enough with the bluffs to know that the ledges above the trail were off-limits to hikers, with warning signs posted about in various languages, warning adventurers of the deadly hazards of venturing up the crumbling sides.

Ruby leaned past his arm just as the skittering clouds sped past the moon, sending silvery rays streaming down upon them. Suddenly Galen could see Ruby's pursed lips so near his face, her eyes darting from trail to cliff, alert, tense.

Beautiful.

Galen realized it didn't matter if they were supposed to meet Rocco somewhere on the trail in the next few minutes. They were on the trail. They were where they'd said they'd be. Rocco could find them.

He needed to talk to Ruby about the kiss they'd shared.

The distant sound of crunching gravel reminded him that Linus and the captain would be following them, might already be close behind them, and could overhear anything Galen might say. Still, he had to say something. He'd just have to be careful that he didn't give away too much. "Ruby?"

"Hmm?"

"Are you okay?"

Her eyes met his, reflecting the silvery light of the moon. Like the one-way glass of the interrogation room, she could see out, but he couldn't see in.

His attention fully on her face, Galen startled when a line swished past the edge of his field of vision. He turned and tried to focus. A rope dangled from the dangerous cliffs above, swishing back and forth as it settled from being flung.

More gravel pattered down along with larger rocks.

Galen pulled Ruby tighter against the cliff face, praying the ledge above would provide them adequate cover against the stones raining down. Ruby's heartbeat hammered beneath his hands, her fright so pronounced he could feel it in her back through her shirt.

The rope moved, thrashing this way and that like a long snake twitching in the throes of death. Something blunt appeared below the lip of the cliff. It swung near them, and Galen jerked away, ducking protectively over Ruby as a second object appeared.

Boots.

On legs.

An instant later a hefty man let go of the rope, dropping to the trail in front of them, landing on his feet. He looked at them, his scarred face in a grin, an instant before the clouds swept across the moon, blocking the light.

"Rocco," Galen greeted the man, though he could no longer see him.

So he didn't see the arm that moved, the hand that grabbed him roughly as the big man spoke. "This way. Hurry."

FOURTEEN

"Climb up." Rocco shoved the rope into her hands.

Ruby looked upward into the darkness. She wasn't dressed for rock climbing—there hadn't been a moment to change clothes, barely time to grab a sandwich from the palace kitchen, with everything that had happened that day. She still wore the same skirt she'd worn to church.

"I—I don't know how," she confessed.

Rocco grunted unhappily, but dropped the rope and tugged them farther down the trail. "You can't see as well from here. Up is better." He paused a few times, moving, darting about in the darkness. The man appeared to be looking toward the marina, searching for something. Finally he stopped. "Here."

Cold metal pressed into her hands. It took Ruby a moment to realize Rocco had handed her a pair of binoculars. "There. Luxury motor yacht, third from the end. Light on in the salon—you can see straight through. See them?"

Ruby struggled to focus the unfamiliar binoculars, to find the spot where Rocco wanted her to look.

"I see the boat." Galen spoke beside her ear, his voice infinitely more gentle than Rocco's harsh tone, his guiding hand welcome as he pointed with one hand, steering the binoculars with the other until they aimed at the boats in the marina. "I can't make out anything of the occupants from this distance."

"Sorry. Only one pair of binoculars, and I want Ruby to recognize them before they go below."

"Who?" Ruby asked. She could see human figures now and cranked the adjustment to focus on their features. Pale hair. Broad shoulders. Big guys sitting at a table, its surface blocked by the galley window. An instant later she had the answer to her own question. "Vincent Verretti. And Carlton."

"And their parents, Milton and Roxanne," Rocco added. "Can you guess why?"

Confused, Ruby admitted, "I can't imagine."

"I felt the same way two years ago when I saw a checked baggage tag on Vincent's backpack as he walked across campus just after spring break. The tag said SFO, clear as day."

"SFO?" Galen repeated in a whisper. "That's an acronym for a U.S. airport?"

"Yup. San Francisco International."

Ruby's thoughts flew. She'd just analyzed the list of Bulldog Bandit heists with the guards. The dates and places were fresh in her mind, along with the corresponding gaps in the school schedule. Spring Break. San Francisco. She leaned against Galen's arm, which was still steady around her shoulder.

Rocco continued, "I asked Vincent where he'd been for spring break, pretended I hadn't already read the tag."

"What did he say?" Ruby asked, her mouth dry.

"He told me, 'nowhere,' and kept walking. When he reached the end of the block he pulled the tag off his bag and threw it away. Now I'm sure lots of folks traveled to San Francisco for spring break, but how many of them care about jewelry? And how many of them don't want to admit where they've been?"

"Can I see?" Galen whispered near her ear, his hand moving to the binoculars.

"Please." Ruby gave them up happily. She'd already seen more than she wanted to see. Rocco hadn't come out and said anything yet, but Ruby could see in the pieces he'd laid out the finished product, just as clearly as she could visualize Stasi's jewelry from a quick study of her design notes.

But this picture wasn't nearly so pretty.

"I'd heard about the Great Bay jewelry heist, and I knew they'd raised the reward for the Bulldog Bandits the moment they found the hairs at the scene of the crime. So I did a little digging," Rocco continued. "Did you know the Verrettis' summer home is right next door to Roxanne's parents' house? And do you know what her mother does for a living?"

Ruby had never been to the Verrettis' house. "What?"

"She raises English Bulldogs. As it turns out, Milton and Roxanne used to own four bulldogs, but they got rid of their beloved pets shortly after hairs were found at the scene of the third jewelry heist, and the phrase 'Bulldog Bandits' was coined."

Galen handed the binoculars back to Ruby. "So the Verrettis are the Bulldog Bandits—and they're here for the Lydian crown jewels."

"Do you think so?" Rocco's tone was sarcastic. "I thought I was your top suspect."

"I'm sorry about that." Galen shifted next to her, and Ruby could feel his frustration with their situation. "We can stop them."

"Two years," Rocco reminded them. "I've been on their trail for two years, gathering evidence until I had something more solid than a few dog hairs and a hunch. If it weren't for me, you wouldn't know who was after your jewelry or your girlfriend."

"We owe you," Galen admitted openly, not reacting to the way the scarred man had referred to Ruby. "You'll get full credit for everything you've done to help us."

The moon cleared the rim of the clouds, and Ruby could see a smile spread across Rocco's face. He wasn't an entirely unpleasant man, once she got past fearing for her life in his presence.

But could they trust him, or was this a trap? Carlton had told her that Luciano Salvatore—aka Rocco—was after the Lydian jewels. Maybe the Verrettis had a noble reason for being in Lydia. Maybe they were there to help her, to save the Lydian jewels from Rocco. She'd known the Verrettis for her entire life. Her parents knew and trusted them.

"How do we know?" Ruby asked, interrupting the men.

"What?" Rocco turned to her as the clouds peeled back from the moon entirely.

This time the moonlight was brighter, the shadows under Rocco's scar that much deeper. Creepy.

Ruby didn't know who to trust. "Carlton Verretti told me you were in Lydia for the crown jewels."

Rocco's smile disappeared. "When did you talk to him?"

"We chatted online yesterday." She realized when she said it that Carlton couldn't have gotten to Lydia since then, not if he wasn't already in the immediate area. But if he was near Lydia, why hadn't he mentioned it during their chat?

"Tell me exactly what was said." Rocco's words were hushed, his voice intense, not threatening…almost afraid.

"I asked him if he'd seen you recently. I—I saw you near Stasi's studio yesterday. I told him as much."

"You told him I'm in Lydia?" The would-be bounty hunter sounded as though he'd been punched. His eyes closed, absorbing her words like the pain of a blow to the stomach.

"I said I thought I'd seen you."

Rocco shook his head. "He knows I'm here. And he knew enough to point the finger of blame at me. He must have guessed I'm after him."

Ruby wasn't completely following all the wild leaps Rocco's reasoning had taken. "He said you were here for the Lydian jewels," she repeated.

"*He's* here for the crown jewels of Lydia." Rocco looked out over the marina and shook his head.

"He said you were."

Rocco turned his face to her, anger snarling from his scar to his lips. "I'm not after the jewels, I'm after the thief. He told you I'm after the jewels so you'd catch me and pull me off his trail—so he could do the job without me catching him."

Ruby stepped back into Galen, who clasped his arm around her protectively. Reassured by his strength behind her, Ruby tried to sort out the conflicting messages she'd gotten from Rocco and Carlton. One of them had to be the guilty party.

Which man should she trust? She closed her eyes and prayed for guidance and clarity as fear pounded through her, its loud hammering drowning out her thoughts.

"You told the Verrettis that I'm in Lydia." Rocco reviewed the facts through his anger. "Carlton's been suspicious of me ever since he saw me detain Nickel the day I turned him in."

"Professor Nickel." Ruby still didn't understand the instructor's role in the events. "You turned him in for a reward?"

"He was wanted for his role in a diamond smuggling operation. I tracked him all the way from Canada."

"The school never told us why he disappeared."

"They didn't want to admit they'd hired a wanted criminal, even if he'd hidden his real identity."

"But Carlton knew who Nickel really was?"

"I don't know. Carlton saw me talking to Nickel and saw the cops later. I tried to keep my name out of the news, but considering the Verrettis' criminal connections, he could have heard about the capture and put the clues together. Both of the brothers gave me wide berth after that, but it didn't matter. I was already on to them."

The story made sense. The pieces fit.

Galen spoke from behind her. "What difference does it make if the Verrettis know who you are and that you're after them?"

"They like to take their time planning a job, work out every possible detail with a contingency plan far ahead of time. That's why they never get caught, never even set off an alarm." Rocco's face slid into darkness as the clouds slipped over the moon once again. "But if they know I'm on to them…"

Ruby raised the binoculars again and focused on the faces of the men inside the boat. They were discussing something, their expressions stern, their eyes narrowed, focused…

"They've got to be deciding whether the heist is worth the risk." Rocco's deep voice echoed off the cliffs in spite of his low volume. The wind caught the words and flung them back, chilling Ruby's spine.

She shivered.

Galen's arm tightened securely around her. "They've invested so much planning into this job. Would they really walk away from it?"

"It's either that, or they get desperate and greedy."

"Desperate." Ruby caught the word and examined it for any hint of hope. "Desperate enough to make a mistake?"

"Desperate enough to act sooner than they'd intended. They know the heat is on. They've had since yesterday to turn and run, but they're still here."

"Then we need to make the first move." Galen sounded determined.

Even as he spoke, Ruby watched through the binoculars as the Verretti men leaned back and laughed, their faces confident.

Something didn't fit. Somebody was lying.

Ruby decided to find out who it was.

"We need to go after them." Galen guided Ruby back down the trail toward Seaview Drive, moving slowly in the darkness. "Rocco has enough evidence to bring them in. We can't wait for them to strike first."

"But I thought the royal guard only has jurisdiction on royal property. You have to wait for them to come after the jewels before you can act."

"Rocco said he can prove they're the Bulldog Bandits."

"Yes, but can he prove they were after the Lydian crown jewels?"

Galen felt his heart fall. He had to catch the jewel thieves to keep his job and help restore the honor of the royal guard. He couldn't let the bandits get away with the crown jewels. His palms itched, eager to strike out before the bandits struck first.

"Something's not right."

"What do you mean?" Galen almost stumbled in the darkness on the uneven trail. The clouds had grown thicker, obscuring the moon's light completely. He caught himself.

Ruby paused, turning back to him in the darkness. "Rocco's story. This whole thing with the jewel thieves, with Isabelle's jewelry. It's all wrong."

"Stealing is always wrong," Galen agreed softly as Ruby remained silent.

"The Verrettis own a chain of jewelry stores. They sell new jewelry, not historical artifacts. The Bulldog Bandits are just the opposite. And where do Stasi's replicas fit in? Who stole the designs, and how did they get them?"

The darkness was too deep for Galen to see Ruby's face, but he heard the confusion and regret in her words and pulled her closer, settling her against his chest. They still hadn't had a chance to discuss their kiss, and knowing that the captain was waiting for them somewhere along the trail, Galen didn't dare raise the issue now. But given the darkness, he figured he could safely hold her without getting caught.

Besides, she sounded so sorrowful he couldn't stand it.

"How are the replica sales going? Have you talked to your father?"

Ruby shook her head, moving his shirt with the slight

motion. "It was the middle of the night back home when I left for church this morning. I tried to catch him this afternoon, but he didn't answer his phone. Probably busy filling orders—I hope."

"I hope so, too." Galen didn't know enough about the jewelry business to offer her any more reassurance than that.

"I want to call them."

Ruby's words came out of nowhere.

"Call who? Your parents?"

"The Verrettis. Somebody's lying, either Rocco or Carlton. Their stories don't match."

"What good will it do to call Carlton? If he's guilty, he'll only lie to you again, and if he suspects you—" Galen tightened his arms protectively around her.

"He didn't say where he was when we chatted yesterday. I didn't think to ask."

"So, you think—"

"I'll ask him where he is. If he denies being in Lydia, I'll know he's been lying to me."

"What if he admits it? What then?"

Ruby hesitated.

Galen couldn't let her put herself in harm's way. "Don't let him know you're on to him. He's already attacked you."

"Are you sure that was him?"

"Does he smoke?"

"A lot of people smoke—something like a quarter of the earth's population. They can't all be suspects."

"So he smokes?" Galen wasn't sure why he wanted the Verrettis to be guilty. Because he wanted answers? Or because he felt jealous of them for sharing Ruby's world? Ever since she'd first mentioned them, Galen had caught a distinct vibe, a note in her voice that struck him wrong. Was there something more between her and the Verrettis, a deeper history that justified his jealousy? Or was he being paranoid?

"Yes, their whole family smokes."

"You can't call them." Galen made up his mind firmly.

"We need answers."

"At what cost? They've already come after you. If they know you suspect them, what will they do? The Bulldog Bandits shoot guards in the back of the head before they can sound an alarm. If these guys think you're going to sound an alarm—"

"They won't hurt me." Ruby took half a step back, out of his arms.

"How do you know that?"

"Remember my first summer in Lydia? I had a boyfriend back home?"

Galen felt as though he'd been slapped. His face stung, panicked, painful. So he hadn't been paranoid. There was something there. He guessed her words before she spoke them, wished he could deny them and make them untrue. "No."

Ruby's voice sounded from far away. She'd continued down the trail without him in the darkness. "Vincent Verretti was my boyfriend. Even when I broke up with him, he said he'd always love me. He won't hurt me. He'll tell me the truth."

FIFTEEN

"I didn't realize how time-consuming being a bridesmaid was going to be," Stasi confessed as she stacked thick files on Ruby's outstretched arms. "I'm not going to have any time for design work this week, but it works out perfectly since we need to move everything from the studio to the safety of the palace." The princess looked at her over the rising stack of files. Ruby could see how overwhelmed her friend felt. "You're sure you don't mind overseeing the move?"

"I'll be fine." Ruby told herself it wasn't a lie. Anyway, Stasi had plenty on her mind already. She needed to feel confident that her studio was in safe hands. Ruby owed her friend that much, at least.

"Is that too much?" Stasi asked, settling another file on the stack, which had grown to cover Ruby's eyes.

"I've got it." Ruby lowered her arms far enough so she could see. Now to walk without dropping anything. At least she only had to make it to the other end of the palace. She took a few unsteady steps toward the door. "No problem. Enjoy yourself this week—it's your sister's wedding. Don't think about the designs or the studio. Everything will be fine."

"Thank you so much, Ruby," the princess called after her.

"No problem," Ruby repeated, trying to convince herself she believed the words.

Galen had been waiting in the hall. He stepped forward silently and reached for the stack of files.

"I've got it," Ruby protested. But even as she spoke, the toe of her shoe caught on the edge of the thick rug that ran the length of the hallway. She careened forward.

Galen caught her and the files, somehow kept the contents from slipping from their folders, and stood her back upright. He kept the files in his arms, carrying her burden for her, but wouldn't meet her eyes.

Didn't speak.

Hadn't spoken to her since they'd returned to the safety of the palace walls the night before, except for one word, spoken with an eyebrow lifted in accusation. They'd relayed all they'd learned to the captain, who'd seemed so frustrated and upset that Ruby hadn't told him about her idea to call the Verrettis. Nor did she share her long-ago relationship status. It didn't seem any more relevant now than it ever had. She'd put Vince Verretti behind her years ago and expected him to stay in the past.

But the past had caught up with her.

It was all her fault. She was the weak link. The Bulldog Bandits might never have known about the Lydian crown jewels if she hadn't traveled to Lydia and drawn their eyes to the tiny kingdom.

Ruby led the way to the empty third-floor suite that was soon to be transformed into Stasi's studio. Galen met her eyes for the briefest second as she unlocked the door.

Betrayal.

She could see it in the pain in his eyes, could hear it in his silence. The word her father had used to accuse her years before echoed forward in time, haunting her. But this time it was so much worse. Had she drawn the bandits to Lydia? She'd known them the longest. She was their only link to the tiny country, besides the time they'd shared in the classroom with

Stasi. If she'd told Galen about Vincent years before, would it have made any difference?

Familiar.

The word replayed in her thoughts as it had since Galen had left it lingering in the air between them the night before, sharply edged like a many-faceted diamond, able to cut through anything, severing all that had held them together.

Familiar. She'd said herself, her attacker seemed familiar.

Should she have recognized him? It wasn't Rocco, she was sure of that. Nor was it Vincent. She'd have recognized him, remembered him sooner. And anyway, he wouldn't be stupid enough to come after her himself, not after the time she'd spent in his arms, albeit years before.

No, but it could have been Carlton or Milton, their father. Just familiar enough to remind her of a long-ago something, but not memorable enough for her to recognize them. It could have been, but it could just as likely have been an associate of Rocco's, or someone else entirely.

Determined to find the answer, she made the same request Galen had denied the night before. "I want to call the Verrettis. Maybe they have a perfectly innocent reason for being near Lydia. Maybe they can explain."

"And maybe they'll hurt you. I won't risk that." Galen set the files on the empty table that occupied the center of the room.

Ruby hurried to the stack and began transferring them folder by folder into the cabinet where they belonged. She mulled over her thoughts, no longer so certain that Vincent wouldn't hurt her, as she'd claimed. She didn't want to think that he was one of the bandits, but she'd had time to mull over her memories. One thing was certain. "I'm sorry I ever dated Vincent."

Galen sagged, deflated, like a pierced balloon falling from the sky, as though her mention of the man had stabbed him between the lungs. If she hadn't been dating Vincent when she'd first met Galen, their lives might be very different. "It's okay that you dated him. He belongs in your world, your country. The jewelry stores, money—"

"I don't care about his stores or his money. My father had always said we'd make a good match, always talked about merging the chains if we married. I admit, the only reason I agreed to date Vincent was because I wanted to win back my father's approval after he accused me of betraying his business."

"Then why did you break up with him?" Galen had his face turned toward the ceiling, away from her, but his voice held more compassion than accusation, and his Adam's apple bobbed anxiously.

"I didn't like him," she confessed in a whisper. "I didn't like who I was when I was with him, and I—" Her breath caught as she realized the truth. "I'd met you by then."

Galen dipped his head and met her eyes.

Ruby knew she shouldn't let on how much he meant to her—how much he'd always meant to her. The man had the power to make her want to stay in Lydia. But she'd deal with the pain of leaving later. Right now she needed to regain the trust of her friend.

"When I was with you," Ruby mustered up a whisper, but her throat felt too tight to manage more, "I felt more protected and cared for than I did when I was with my boyfriend. For the first time I realized that jewelry and gifts don't equal love. I didn't want to be with him. I wanted—" Ruby's throat tightened, cutting off her words. She wished Galen would move toward her, open his arms to her, pull her close and tell her everything was going to be okay.

But he took a step away, toward the door. "Come with me."

"Where?"

"We're going to call the Verrettis."

It was the same setup they'd used when Galen had taken the call from Rocco. Ruby would make the call from a private room, visible through two-way glass, while the call was broadcast in the conference room for the guards to analyze. Meanwhile, the cell phone officials would ping back the wireless connection to the area towers to pinpoint the Verrettis' location, cross-checking whether the family was where they claimed to be.

Galen had interrupted a lecture from the spiky-haired wedding planner to get Captain Selini's approval.

The captain had looked grateful for the excuse to send the woman away, with his promise to return the guards to wedding practice as soon as Stasi's studio contents had been safely moved.

Now Galen sat next to the captain at the conference table while Ruby punched in the phone number Carlton had given her when they had chatted online two days before.

With each ring, Galen felt his tension rise, until he feared the Verrettis wouldn't answer at all.

"Hello?" The voice sounded distinctly American and vaguely annoyed.

"This is Ruby Tate. I'm looking for—"

"This is Milton. Did you want to talk to Vince?"

Ruby hesitated. The plan had been to talk to Carlton. "Actually, Carlton and I were chatting the other day..." Ruby's voice trailed off as Milton, ignoring her, shouted.

"Hey, Vince, your girlfriend's on the phone."

Girlfriend? Galen felt Selini's eyes on him, but he couldn't look away from Ruby's face, which had gone nearly the color of her hair. Was she still secretly dating Vince, in spite of her claim that they'd broken up four years before? Galen didn't want to believe it, and yet Ruby didn't correct anyone or press to talk to Carlton instead.

"Hey, baby." Vincent's voice sounded affectionate, eager. "I'm so glad you called."

"You—you are?"

"I've been thinking about you. Where are you these days?"

Ruby's mouth hung open, frantic questions in her eyes as she looked at the guards through the glass for guidance on how to respond.

The captain wrote quickly, filling a piece of paper with one word, holding it up for her to see.

"Lydia," she read.

"That's right, good old Lydia. Hey, I saw the Tate Jewelry royal wedding line got scooped." He gave a low whistle. "That's got to hurt."

"No, it's fine. We're fine, actually." Ruby chirped in a voice too high, too perky to pass for her own. "The news picked up the story so it's like free advertising." The laugh didn't sound like her natural laugh, either.

"It's okay, Ruby. I understand." Vincent called her bluff. "And I'm here for you. My offer still stands."

"I don't—" Ruby shook her head, then nodded as she read the sign the captain held, "Where are you?"

"Where am I?"

"Mmm-hmm."

"I'm in a good place. Verretti Jewels is in a good place."

"I mean geographically."

"Ah, actually we're in your neighborhood."

"You are?"

"Yeah, the whole family is on the yacht in the Mediterranean."

"Really?" Ruby looked almost relieved, read Selini's sign, nodded again. "Where in the Mediterranean?"

"Near Sicily."

Ruby froze. "Are you sure?"

"Yep, right near Sicily—that's off the eastern coast of the Italian mainland, you know."

"Yeah, I know. So, everybody's well? You're all well?" Ruby chatted with Vince for several more minutes nodding politely when he told her about his father's golfing obsession and his mother's devotion to animal charities.

"That's right, I recall she had pet dogs. What breed was that?"

"Boxers."

"Boxers?"

"Yes, rare white boxers. She was quite proud of them. Sadly they were poisoned a few years ago, just after you and I broke up."

"I'm so sorry. I need to be going," Ruby sent her greetings to the rest of Vince's family before ending the call. She looked shaken as she joined the guards in the conference room.

The captain leaned far back in his chair and blew out a long breath toward the ceiling. "Were they really white boxers?"

"I don't know. I'm not sure I know the difference, and that was years ago," Ruby apologized. "Do you think he was lying to throw us off his trail?"

"He lied about one thing." Captain Selini laid his tablet flat on the table so that everyone could see the screen. "He's not near Sicily. The ping-backs tracked him to the Sardis marina."

Galen looked at the map, which was zoomed in to show a blinking arrow above the area of the marina where the Verretti yacht had been docked the night before. "So now what? Do we move in?"

"What do we have on them? Attempted kidnapping?" The captain gestured to Ruby. "Can she identify them this time?"

"I can," Ruby agreed.

"And Rocco Salvatore, your bounty hunter friend—are we certain he has enough evidence to convict? These people are American citizens. If we can't hold them, I don't want to touch them."

Galen met Ruby's eyes. She'd heard every word Rocco had said to them the night before, and she'd known Rocco a lot longer than he had.

"Call Rocco," Ruby suggested. "Can he meet you at the marina?"

"If we're going to go after them, we should go now." Galen

knew that much for certain. "Before they have time to won-
der why Ruby called out of the blue."

Captain Selini instructed Oliver, who'd been handling the
connection between Ruby's phone and the conference room,
to put through the call. Galen took his place on the other side
of the two-way glass, holding the phone.

Thankfully, Rocco answered quickly.

"Where are you right now?" Galen asked without pre-
amble.

"Watching the marina."

"Good." He'd be able to reach the boat quickly, then.

"Not so good."

"Why not?"

"The Verrettis just cast off."

"What do you mean?"

"They sailed away. They're gone."

"Can you see them?"

A straining noise, as if he was checking to be sure. "No,
not anymore."

"Do you know where they're headed? Could we go after
them?"

"They went around an island. You Lydians have a lot of
islands out here."

"I know." Galen closed his eyes to the disappointed faces
on the other side of the glass. "Can you watch for them and
call us when they come back?"

"Sure thing. If they return, this will be the first number
I call."

Two days later, as Galen arrived early for his Wednes-
day evening shift outside the emptying studio, Rocco finally called.

"Found them."

"Where?"

"Docked in the shallows off the coast, north of the city."

"Can we move in?"

"They're not there."

"What do you mean?"

"I mean there's nobody on the boat. They left." As Rocco spoke, Galen scanned the street, the sidewalk, the men, royal guards working alongside professional movers, passing by carrying boxes to a waiting truck.

And Ruby. She stood with her back to him, clipboard in hand, darting from man to man checking the stickers on each box, consulting her list, nodding and checking things off. Galen hadn't wanted her to help with the move, but she'd insisted she owed it to the princess after the way she'd betrayed the royal jewels.

"Are they coming back?"

"I imagine so. But I think the bigger question is, what are they doing on the mainland? They stayed away for two days, why come back now? What's so important?"

Galen kept his eyes on Ruby. Another box-toting man approached her. A big man, his face mostly obscured by a low hat, beard and sunglasses. But when Ruby looked from his box to his face, she stuttered back, mouth open and turned to run away.

"I think I know," Galen said, mostly to himself as he dived across the sidewalk toward Ruby, just as the big guy got his arms around her, hauling her toward the curb as an unmarked van swerved to meet them, door open, not even stopping as the man shoved Ruby inside.

SIXTEEN

Ruby hooked one foot against the doorframe and pushed back, fighting against the arms that held her as Carlton Verretti shoved her through the van door.

Her resistance might not have meant much, except that Carlton suddenly tipped backward, letting go of her as he turned to face the guard who'd jumped him.

"Run!" Galen shouted as he tackled Carlton from the back, handcuffs ready as he struggled against the bigger man.

Ruby saw it all in one blink as she tore past them toward the safety of the studio door. Confused men from the moving company shuffled in front of her, blocking her way.

One of them reached for her, and Ruby recognized Vincent under sunglasses and a fake beard. She screamed as she leaped in the other direction. From the corner of one eye, she saw Paul and Sam, the two royal guards who'd been on duty all day.

"No!" Ruby screamed, trying to warn them away as Vincent drew his gun.

She ducked to the side, tripped over the box Carlton had dropped, and tried to scramble over it when Vincent grabbed her around the waist. His gun, eerily quiet, sent bullets spitting against the limestone walls, a barrier of death between her and the guards rushing to her aid.

"No!" She beat against Vincent's arm, kicked backward,

thrashing, hoping to hit his knee or anything more than the empty air that met her every effort. Twisting, flailing, she tried to pry his fingers loose as he bounded over the fallen boxes toward the van, taking her with him.

Blood coursed down Galen's face. He'd gotten one cuff on Carlton's arm, but now Milton and Carlton had him between them, pummeling him back through the open van door as the vehicle crept down the block, gaining speed. Vince's father and brother hurled Galen in through the van door, then jumped inside after him.

Paul and Sam hurtled the obstacle course of boxes and ran after the vehicle, close enough to grab the rear bumper but unable to do anything to stop the accelerating van.

Vincent raised his gun as he kept pace with the retreating vehicle.

Still caught in Vincent's viselike grip, Ruby lunged toward the weapon, hands swatting, fingers clawing as she did everything she could to disrupt the shots.

Windows shattered high above them, raining down glass as Vincent's shots went wild. He flung Ruby through the van door and joined her, slamming the door shut behind him, blocking out the light.

Ruby landed on her back next to something bumpy and wet. She tried to peel herself away, to scramble toward the back door of the van, but Carlton had her by the arm. She swept her other hand back into something sticky...

Galen's face.

He didn't move, didn't open his eyes. Ruby froze, praying with every beat of her heart that they hadn't killed him. His breath, faint as a whisper, warmed her cold fingers.

He was alive. For now.

The contents of his stomach surged, sloshing, threatening to escape. His head throbbed. Darkness, thick like a down-filled blanket, pressed against him, against his heaving stomach and pounding head.

His mouth felt dry, rusty. Tasted rusty. Blood.

There were smells, too. The smell of his blood, near but not overpowering. The scent of the sea, but closer still something dank and moldering. And tar. He sniffed again, recognizing it finally. Old baked-in cigarette smoke.

Where was he?

Where was Ruby?

Concern shot through him. He tried to open his eyes, stopped when he felt the resistance of dried blood caked in his lashes. Pain in his shoulder and neck told him he'd been lying on his side far too long.

Galen flexed his fingers. They brushed against something…something soft.

"Are you awake?" Ruby's voice sounded dry.

"Unh," Galen tried to answer, nearly gagged on the blood pooled in his mouth, swallowed past his thick tongue. He remembered more now. He'd bitten his tongue when Carlton had slugged him in the jaw—that was the ache in the side of his face. He cleared his throat enough to speak. "Are you okay?"

"More okay than you are." She sounded weary, too.

"Where are we?"

"On a boat, somewhere deep below deck. The engine room, maybe? I don't know any more than that. From the feel of it, we've been sailing all night."

"Is it night?" Galen had eased his eyes open at last, only to discover he couldn't see anything more with them open than he had with them closed.

"I don't know. I'm assuming. I dozed for a while, but I must have sat here for hours before that." She sniffled at the reminder of her vigil.

Galen could imagine the fear she'd felt. He felt it now, rising inside him. Where were the Verrettis taking them? What were their plans? How long would they let them live?

He had to get Ruby off the boat, get her to safety, contact the royal guard.

As if reading his mind, Ruby offered, "They took our cell phones."

Of course. Galen flexed his shoulders and found his arms bound at the wrists behind him. His legs, when he tried to move them, proved to be tied together, secured to something immobile near his feet. "Can you move?"

"I'm handcuffed to a metal bar. Whatever it is, it won't budge and it's bolted to something big on either end."

Slowly, painfully, Galen assessed their mobility, finally resigning himself to the Verrettis' upper hand. He and Ruby weren't going anywhere. They could hardly move.

"You were right," Galen admitted as their situation sunk in.

"About?"

"The Verrettis. They're the ones who attacked you, not Rocco."

"Do you think Rocco's really a bounty hunter? Or an accomplice trying to distract us?"

"I was on the phone with Rocco when Carlton grabbed you." Pain speared through his head, down his neck, as Galen fought for clarity through the fog. Had Rocco called him to distract him while Carlton made his move?

Ruby's voice cut through his thoughts. "What do you think they're going to do with us?"

"Use us to get the crown jewels."

"And then?"

"Who says we're going to let them get that far?"

"I don't think we have a choice. All they need is my handprint. They don't care about having my permission to use it."

Galen heard the fear and the strain in her voice. He could imagine what she'd been thinking, lying in the darkness mostly alone. If she fought them, made it difficult for them to use her handprint in a stealthy way, or acted like she might try to sound the alarm, they didn't have any reason to let her live. They'd get the crown jewels, regardless.

The inescapable reality swirled uneasily in his gut with every rise and fall of the boat. The Verrettis' plan couldn't fail. Even if Captain Selini decided to post a guard by the vault, the Verrettis would simply shoot the men and take what they wanted. They'd never triggered an alarm on a heist before.

They'd never left anyone alive who could describe them.

A sliver of light cut through the darkness, marking the outline of the door. Someone had turned on a light outside the room. Were they coming for them? Galen struggled to think clearly through the pain.

"Whatever happens," he told Ruby, "I want you to trust me. I'm going to get you out of this, but we might have to make some sacrifices."

"Sacrifices?"

Galen pinched his eyes shut. He hated the choice he was being forced to make, hated knowing what it would mean. "We have to cooperate with them."

"No. I'm not—"

"Then they'll kill you. They'll kill us both."

"I don't care. I'm *not* going to betray my friend."

"You'll betray her either way." The truth tore through him, somehow even worse when he spoke the words out loud. "They'll proceed without your permission."

"I'll fight them. I'll resist." From the sound of Ruby's voice, Galen guessed she was crying again, could picture wet tears streaming down her cheeks in the darkness.

"They're not going to risk that. They'll use your handprint by force or kill you." Galen dropped his words to a whisper when something echoed in the hallway outside, a loud hollow sound that could mean anything. He strained to hear.

"So if we cooperate, then what?" Ruby whispered after they waited several tense minutes and no one appeared.

"They'll get away with the crown jewels and shoot us dead, maybe shoot a bunch of other people, too. They won't leave us alive. I looked up the heist stories yesterday. Do you know their total body count? Seventeen. They've killed seventeen people that we know of, plus who knows how many whose bodies were never found? It won't matter. If we resist, they won't know the code to open the vault door, or the glass cases. They'll trigger an alarm and get caught."

"If the guards rush them in the vault, what do you think will happen?" Galen thought of his fellow guards entering the tight space, the Verrettis hiding behind the bulletproof cases with every advantage. "They'll be shot. They'll pick them off as they come in the door. It's a death trap. If we're going to stop them, it's got to be outside of the vault. Lives or jewels. That's the choice."

"So you think we should give away the jewels? Will that save our lives?"

"Will resisting save the jewels? We don't know how much they know. They know the frequency for the royal guard ear-pieces—who knows how much they've been listening in, or how long they've been planning this? They could know everything. How did they know to come after you? We can't underestimate how much they already know."

Ruby sniffled. "I'm still not telling them anything. I won't betray my friend."

Another hollow thud echoed through the hallway. Galen had yet to hear footsteps, but something was definitely happening not far past their door. Fear burned through him with urgency. He had to make Ruby understand. It was going to be difficult enough to keep her alive, even with her full participation. If she didn't trust him, they wouldn't stand a chance.

"I'm a Lydian Royal Guard, Ruby." Galen let the pride and honor carry through past the pain in his voice. "I have pledged my life to keep safe the royal family and royal property. I would die before I let the Bulldog Bandits get their hands on the crown jewels. But I know one thing with utter certainty. I would sooner watch them empty the vault than let them hurt you."

The room fell completely silent as Ruby's crying stopped. "You can't choose that. You have to protect the crown jewels."

But Galen had made up his mind. They were outnumbered, outmaneuvered, trapped. If he tried to save everything—the jewels and Ruby and himself—he'd end up losing it all. But if he could pick just one thing, and focus on saving that one thing, he might have a chance. And as long as there was a chance, Galen would do everything in his power to save that one thing, even if it meant losing everything else.

"I'm going to get you out of this, Ruby, but you've got to trust me and do exactly as I say. Can you do that?"

Silence.

"Ruby?"

Her heart resisted Galen's words, her father's accusations running through her head, his rebuttal ready the moment she'd made her defense.

I would never do anything to betray the jewelry stores.

Maybe not knowingly, but you still betrayed us. You betrayed us without even realizing it. Gregory Tate had spoken out of anger—Ruby knew that. He'd later apologized for his harsh words, but he'd never taken them back. Because deep down, he truly believed she'd let them all down.

Just like she was letting down Stasi right now. "I don't deserve to be saved," Ruby told Galen finally.

But her words were obscured by a rhythmic booming in the hallways outside, followed by a rattling of keys and finally a grating squeal as the steel door swung open and the light flashed on, blinding her with its sudden brightness.

Ruby closed her eyes against the burning light, then raised them slightly, just enough to see Galen lying bound in front of her, bloodied, bruised, hurting.

His request echoed through her thoughts. *I'm going to get you out of this, Ruby, but you've got to trust me and do exactly as I say.*

With sudden clarity, she realized she trusted him, even more than she trusted herself. "Galen?" She whispered his name as the large shadow in the doorway moved closer. "I'll do whatever you say."

An evil laugh bellowed above her. "What's that, Ruby? Making promises you can't keep? Don't bother talking to this guard. He's as good as dead."

"You need him!" Ruby had adjusted to the light enough to look Vincent full in the face.

"Not by my reckoning. Near as I can tell, we just need you."

"You need the codes he has memorized." Ruby thought quickly, realizing that if she told the Verrettis that the codes were the coronation years, they'd find a history book and dump Galen in the sea. No, she had to make them believe Galen was invaluable to their plans.

The royal guard wanted to save her life? She'd save his right back, if she could. And maybe, if they were very fortunate, they could trigger an alarm and save the crown jewels, too.

But one thing at a time.

"You want the crown jewels, don't you?"

"How'd you figure that out? That Salvatore punk tell you all about us? Thought you only cared about the wedding jewels."

"They were just a decoy, weren't they? You stole the designs to distract us." Ruby realized the truth of her words as she spoke them.

Vincent looked slightly surprised, then guilty. Then he laughed. "The whole store's a front, a great excuse to have connections in the jewelry world, to launder anything that might otherwise make folks suspicious. Funny how we Verrettis can run a facade that's more successful than Tate Jewelry will ever be."

His words knocked her breath from her lungs. Ruby wanted

to make a smart retort, but she could hardly inhale past the ache in her chest, feeling her family's failures all the more acutely now.

Vincent had a pistol in one hand, a large hunting knife in the other. He slashed the knife toward Galen's legs.

Ruby screamed.

"Calm down." Vincent brandished the knife at her, waving it uncomfortably close to her face in the belly of the rocking boat. She realized he'd cut Galen's legs free. "Gonna take him upstairs. We'll talk like civilized people."

A rush of hope dizzied her as Vincent pulled her to her feet. Maybe this was their chance. Maybe, if they broke free—

But Carlton appeared in the doorway a moment later and hauled Galen, still mostly bound, to his feet. He shoved him out the door and Vincent shoved her after them. She stumbled up the stairs. As she'd suspected, night had fallen. The moon and stars shone down clearly from the cloudless sky, reminding her of the night she and Galen had watched for falling stars. The island had been nearby, somewhere in the archipelago off the Lydian capital of Sardis, but Ruby didn't know the area well enough to identify their precise location.

Roxanne Verretti waited at the landing with a gun in one hand, a dog leash in the other. Two saggy-eyed bulldogs sat at her feet, the wrinkles of their chins disappearing into the folds of their necks and shoulders. Ruby had never realized how much Roxanne looked like her beloved pets—which obviously hadn't been poisoned. Another lie? Or had the pets simply been replaced?

"We're far enough out to sea," Carlton announced as he hauled Galen toward the starboard side of the yacht and shoved him high against the rail. "How's about I hold him and you shoot him?"

SEVENTEEN

"No!" Ruby's protest came out like a scream.

Galen couldn't hear anything else, but he saw Roxanne Verretti raise her gun and point it his direction. He still wore his body armor under his uniform shirt, but at this close range, she could hit him in the head or neck if she was a decent shot, or wound him and toss him over to die slowly.

Considering that his hands were still bound behind his back, Carlton could toss him over uninjured, and he'd have little chance of making it to shore, never mind that he was a strong swimmer. In fact, if Carlton continued to hold him by his collar, his toes an inch above the deck, he'd strangle him before he ever hit the water.

Roxanne didn't shoot.

It took Galen a moment to see why, and he struggled for each precious breath.

Vincent had extended his hand, palm out, in front of her, like a crossing guard instructing her to stop. "Ruby says we need him."

"You need him," Ruby confirmed in a shaking voice. "He's the only one here who knows the codes."

"You don't know the codes? How's come they give you clearance if you don't know the codes?" Roxanne didn't seem to have a tight grasp on English grammar, but given her grip on the Glock in her hand, Galen doubted she had often been corrected.

"They only tell me the codes for the cases I need, when I need them. If you try to get into the cases without knowing the codes, you'll trigger the alarm."

Roxanne looked from Ruby to Vincent.

Vincent shrugged. "We need codes to override the alarm."

"We need the guard?" Roxanne didn't sound happy about it.

"We need the guard." Carlton didn't sound happy, either, but he lowered his arm.

His feet finally flat on the deck, Galen sucked in a welcome breath and tried to think clearly. They'd averted one crisis. How many more lay ahead?

"Let's sort this out." Vincent hauled Ruby up a few steps into the salon, the same room the Verrettis had occupied when Rocco had pointed them out from the cliffs overlooking the marina.

Carlton shoved Galen in next, and Roxanne followed with her dogs snuffling at her heels. Galen didn't see Milton, but the pilothouse rose above the salon, its lights on low. Probably Vince and Carlton's father was up there, steering the boat.

As his eyes adjusted to the posh salon interior, Galen observed what he hadn't been able to see from the cliffs Sunday night.

The room was the Verrettis' control central, with maps and schedules and electronic equipment spread across the table, scattered over the countertops, piled in the corners on the floor. None of it appeared to be a permanent fixture, which didn't surprise Galen in the least. No doubt the bandits needed to be able to dispose of evidence quickly. At the moment, however, they must have felt secure. There was enough evidence in the room to link them to any number of crimes in Lydia alone.

It was a reminder he didn't need. They wouldn't have let

him and Ruby see the evidence if they had any intention of letting them live long enough to share what they'd seen.

Galen's resolve hardened. He had to help Ruby escape somehow. Eventually Rocco would catch up to the bandits. Someday they'd face justice. But Galen knew Rocco had no intention of going after the Americans until they returned to the US, where he could bring them in without facing any charges himself.

Galen prayed silently for the safety of his fellow guards. For their sakes, he didn't want them anywhere near the vault.

"Here we go." Milton pulled out a hand-drawn map of the old city wall, the hidden steel door and initial passage entrance marked in red. "They put a bunch of extra guards on the old city side of the wall."

Galen felt his heart sink. The royal guards were all expected to be on duty for Isabelle's wedding, so Selini had asked for volunteers to work extra shifts covering the stretch of wall between the information guard booth and the tower known as The Last Stronghold. Since none of the men had been told what they would be guarding, Galen had hoped his fellow guards wouldn't volunteer. Unfortunately, none of the men he worked with had ever been known to back down when help was needed.

From what Milton said, Galen knew his fellow guards had risen to the challenge. Which meant his closest peers would be out in force when the bandits arrived. And the bandits had a history of shooting guards before they ever saw them coming.

He couldn't let the bandits shoot his friends. But as he prayed silently for the safety of his friends, he couldn't help wondering how he was going to keep Ruby safe if he didn't play along.

Milton stabbed a finger at the other side of the map, where a creek meandered through the ancient moat and trees grew thick on the other side of the wall. "We'll approach from outside the old city."

"But there's no entrance on that side," Ruby protested.

"Ain't there?" Milton lit a cigar with a chuckle. "We're going in the tower window." He pointed to The Last Stronghold.

"It's a hundred feet off the ground." Galen informed him bluntly, Kirk's many explanations running through his mind. It was too high. They'd need a helicopter or a crane, but the trees were too thick to allow a crane anywhere near the tower, not that a crane would be remotely stealthy.

Milton leaned back and puffed on his cigar, chuckling as he snapped his fingers at Carlton.

The younger bandit pulled out a large black nylon bag. "Pneumatic line-throwing grappling hook launching system." Carlton's eyebrows danced with excitement as he read off the features from the label. "Self-retractable, capable of towing a 7mm Kevlar line 120 vertical feet, complete with noise-mitigating system."

Milton blew a puff of smoke toward Galen's face. "Sounds like your tower won't be a problem. Now, explain to me why I need you both to get me in there?"

Galen explained, every word feeling like treason on his lips, fear nearly stopping his heart half a dozen times as he realized that he couldn't help them, couldn't get them through all the security measures even if he wanted to.

But each time he hit a roadblock, instead of declaring him worthless and shooting him on the spot, the relentless thieves around the table found a solution to the obstacle. In the end, the Verrettis seemed pleased with their plan. Galen felt sick to his stomach. After going over every step of the plan in scrupulous detail, Galen couldn't see when or how he would trigger an alarm without the bandits knowing or even catch a break to help Ruby escape. He prayed that God would open his eyes, to see his chance when it came. To give him a chance, however small.

The Verrettis' plan was simple. Galen and Ruby would

get them inside the vault and give them access to the jewels. And as soon as the bandits no longer needed their help, they'd eliminate them.

Galen prayed he'd find an opportunity to free Ruby before it came to that.

"Take him back downstairs," Vincent instructed his brother. "Me and Ruby got a lot of catching up to do."

Ruby drew back. "I don't want—"

Vincent silenced her with a slap across the cheek. "You do, babe."

Galen couldn't stand it. He lunged forward, out of Carlton's grip, across the table toward where Vincent sat on the cushy curved bench next to Ruby. He'd told himself to bide his time, to wait for an opening, to wait at least until they were closer to shore or had their arms untied. But there was no more waiting, not if Vincent was going to hurt Ruby right now.

Pushing off with the soles of his feet against the built-in benches that encircled the table, Galen spun a swift half circle on the papers that littered the smooth surface. He dropped down onto the bench, his hands still tied behind his back but able to steady him as he shot his legs straight out. As he got his feet around Vincent's neck, he then slammed Vincent's head against the cushioned seatback, wedging one heel against his forehead, one instep against his neck. Vincent squealed like an angry pig, his eyes bulging.

He saw the butt of the gun moving toward his face a split second before Carlton thumped his temple with a hard blow and everything went dark.

Ruby wanted to scream, to dive across the table after Galen, but Carlton followed his blow by swiftly tugging Galen from the table and dragging him down the stairs.

"Gimme a hand, Ma," Carlton whined as Galen's prone foot caught against the doorframe.

Roxanne kicked the foot free. She'd been puffing on a

cigarette and pulled it out to talk. "I'll get your father. I'm not touching those dirty shoes. I just got my nails done this morning." She ambled down the stairs after her son, the dogs snuffling in her wake, leaving Ruby alone with Vincent.

Ruby tried to inch away from Vincent, but he had one arm tight around her waist and pulled her closer to him instead.

"Don't make me hit you again. I won't be so nice this time," he warned through gritted teeth. "I got a deal for you, a good deal. The only deal you're going to get."

Hardly budging from his spot on the bench, Vince reached back, grabbed a laptop from the counter behind him and flipped it open.

Ruby recognized the document on the screen. They were the income accounts from Tate Jewelry, updated that afternoon. She felt blood rushing dizzily to her head, pounding at her temples. It couldn't be. "How did you—"

"Easy, babe. I planted a remote transmitter inside your father's CPU. I can see everything on his hard drive and everything on his screen."

"When? How?"

"The first time was during your high school graduation party. You made that easy for me. All I had to do was sneak away while you and your friends were playing some stupid game, unlock one pathetic little door lock. Really, if your dad valued his business, you'd think he'd protect it better."

"But my father replaces his computer every two years."

"A nuisance, I admit," Vince clicked through reports, showing expenditures, sales projections, even the latest numbers on the royal wedding jewelry replicas. He closed the page quickly, but not before Ruby saw that the replicas were selling high on their projected range.

In spite of being knocked off. In spite of everything Vincent had done to sabotage her father's business. Ruby felt a heady swirl of hope.

Vincent kept talking. "I just snuck in again and replaced

it. Not a difficult task for someone of my talents." He smiled at her, then, a smile she recognized from years before and had once mistaken for confidence, but now saw as conceit.

He seemed so sure of himself. An ill sense of foreboding crept through her veins.

"Why are you telling me this?" She felt certain he wouldn't let her out of his sight now that she knew what he'd done, not when she knew enough to send him to jail for multiple life sentences.

His smile grew. "I'm a reasonable man, Ruby. I've always liked you." He reached for her face. Drew her closer.

Ruby's spine stiffened, resisting.

"Do you have any idea how wealthy I am?" Vincent's voice went husky. "Your parents want to retire. A merger of Verretti Jewels and Tate Jewelry would be advantageous to us all."

Ruby opened her mouth to ask why, with all his wealth, he'd want to acquire her parents' chain, but she realized the answer before she spoke.

A front, a cover-up. Of course. He'd already told her Verretti Jewels was an excuse for their connections in the jewelry world, a way to launder their illegal activities without arousing suspicions. With twice the stores, they could launder twice as much, spread out, relax and not worry about anyone following a trail straight to them.

"What do you say, Ruby? Merge with me?" He leaned close, the sooty fumes of his breath sticking to her instead of passing by.

Her instinct said to push him away, but with her wrists still bound behind her, that wasn't an option. "Why? What's in it for me?"

"Life."

She shook her head, exhaling through her nostrils, trying to blow his grimy scent away. She didn't believe him. Given what she knew of his illegal activities, he'd be foolish to let her live once the crown jewel heist was complete. Vincent had many faults, but a lack of intelligence wasn't one of them.

Surely the bandit had no intention of letting her live, no matter what he promised. Still, if she had any chance of escaping, of saving Galen or the crown jewels, she needed to stay on Vincent's good side. She'd promised Galen she'd follow his lead, and up until he'd pinned Vince to the seat back, Galen had been playing along.

"What are your terms?"

Vince pulled out a contract, the specifics of the business transaction spelled out clearly. He flipped through the pages so she could see.

"And?" She didn't believe that was all. The terms were too generous, and she doubted Vincent would simply let her go, not when she could run straight to the authorities.

"And you marry me."

Ruby closed her eyes.

Vincent kept talking, his face too close to hers, the tar in his breath thick enough to smother her. "You become one of us. Our crimes become yours, so that if you ever try to bring us down…" He stood, pulled her by the arm along the curve of the bench until she stood on shaky legs free of the table. "You'll bring yourself and your parents down, too."

She wanted to scream, to slap him, to stomp and kick, but she had to play along, wait for an opening. "And if I don't agree?"

"I kill you and your parents."

Ruby opened her eyes, met his, saw no sign of hesitation or mercy there.

Vince continued. "And that guard in the engine room, if he's not dead already."

Galen wasn't dead. Ruby was relieved to see he'd come to, though they'd bound him more securely this time, in a seated position, a chain wrapped around his waist to some massive engine part behind him, besides the cords that bound his wrists and ankles.

Vincent tossed her into the room and slammed the door shut. Keys rattled in the lock, and finally even the sliver of light around the door disappeared along with his retreating footsteps.

"Are you going to be okay?" Ruby stumbled forward and slumped to her knees next to Galen. From what she'd seen before the lights went out, he was beat up pretty bad, fresh blood oozing down the side of his face from his latest injury.

"For now, but they haven't given us anything to eat or drink."

"I don't think they intend for us to live long enough for that to be a problem." Given the approaching sunrise, the bandits had decided to put off the heist until the next night. Ruby hoped they'd get something to drink before then, but based on their treatment so far, she wouldn't expect anything.

With her hands still bound behind her, Ruby had a difficult time assessing Galen's bonds.

"What are you trying to do?" he asked as she slumped against his shoulder. The ship rocked on the waves, pushing her against him. She grabbed at the chain around him to hold herself steady.

"I'm—ouch—trying—" The boat rolled again. Only her grip on his chains kept her from tipping over. "Trying to find a way out of here. Maybe if we incapacitate the engines? Then they'd have to come down here and fix them."

Galen didn't respond.

Ruby feared he'd slipped out of consciousness again. His injuries looked so ugly; they'd hit him so many times. Even she felt worried, hungry, thirsty and exhausted. "Galen?"

"Try it. Try whatever you can. I'd help but…"

"They're more afraid of you than they are of me. They know you'd find a way to get us out of here if one existed."

"I'd do anything." His voice cut out.

The rocking ship sent her closer to him, her face buried in his shoulder. Without use of her arms, it was difficult to move. That, and she didn't really want to be away from him. Exhaustion and fear pulled at her and she sagged down to a seated position next to where he had slumped on the floor. "Remember two summers ago, when you brought our boat back to shore, swimming the entire way?"

"I remember."

"You were amazing."

"I was desperate. And arguably, stupid."

"I've been the stupid one." Ruby felt a tear course down her cheek. Oh, how she wished she could go back in time and change what had happened. But how far back would she go? She'd never have dated Vincent or let him anywhere near her father's office. But what if she'd never met Galen?

Her heart nearly stopped beating at the thought. Galen had saved her life. But her life wouldn't have needed saving if she hadn't crossed paths with the Verrettis. Galen had talked to her about God's love.

It was a memory she didn't want to undo. "Tell me about the stars again," she whispered.

"You can't see them from down here."

"But they're still out there."

"You're right." Galen pulled in a breath. "It was from Isaiah 40:26. God brings out the starry host one by one and calls them each by name."

"He knows their names." Ruby pinched her eyes shut and remembered the stars, so many more stars in those island skies, without any city lights to dim them. Galaxies, billions of stars.

"And God knows." Galen finished the verse. "Not one of them is missing."

God saw all the stars, knew their names, kept track of them. God saw her, too, crouched in the darkness in the yacht's engine room, dirty and afraid. God saw her, and God knew.

The thought warmed her like a tiny spark inside, the glimmer smaller than that of the most distant star. And yet, it was enough to give her hope.

EIGHTEEN

"Don't try anything." Carlton flashed his gun, reminding them, as he had countless times already, that he was prepared to maim or kill them at the slightest provocation.

Galen fought the churning in his gut, the dried out pizza crusts and flat soda the Verrettis had fed them earlier sloshing like the boat beneath his feet. At least he had something to sustain him. They'd even let him use the restroom, his hands free just long enough to splash water on his face and wipe off the worst of the bloodstains.

Dried blood still covered his shirt, sticking to his skin and the sweat from his body armor. Bruises and cuts festered untended on his arms and face. Obviously the Verrettis didn't expect him to be seen.

Night had fallen once again. In spite of their cramped positions chained in the engine room, he and Ruby had slept. His heart warmed at the memory of the way she'd leaned on him, shared her favorite memories with him, even brushed a kiss across his cheek. He'd see she got out of this alive, or die trying.

The Verrettis had docked their yacht on a private pier south of the city. Galen recognized the property and knew the owner traveled extensively on his own boat. Seeing it missing, Galen prayed the man wouldn't get back in time to cross paths with the Verrettis and their guns.

Better that no one crossed paths with them.

Vincent had been missing from the deck, but as they stumbled across the dock toward the waiting SUV, Galen saw the elder brother step out from the driver's side. They'd ditched the van, then—probably figured it had been seen when they'd kidnapped him and Ruby. Where they got this other vehicle, Galen didn't know, but they had nearly unlimited resources at their disposal and clearly had no qualms about stealing, so the new vehicle didn't surprise him at all.

The men tossed him in the back like a piece of luggage. He couldn't see what they did with Ruby, but figuring two bucket seats in front and a bench in the middle, there were just enough places for the four Verrettis plus Ruby to sit. Most likely they planned to put their loot in the spacious back storage compartment where he now lay, which meant there wouldn't be room for him after the heist.

Yet another reminder that they didn't intend for him to survive that long.

The SUV rumbled down a rough road, then turned and glided smoothly along the highway. Galen followed the route in his head, planning how to tell the rest of the guards where to find the Verrettis' yacht, if he got the chance. Soon Galen felt the familiar reverberations of tires on cobblestones, and after some twisting and turning, the vehicle stopped.

Carlton pulled him out, along with a couple bags of gear. Milton set the time on his watch, synchronized to the timer his wife had secured to the dashboard. Roxanne drove away silently; the plan, as Galen understood it, was for her to circle back in fifteen minutes unless they called her sooner, to drive through the park on a wide path to pick them up near the tower. For now, they were to hike in to avoid drawing any attention.

They shuffled down the long path, the trees casting shadows that transformed the peaceful park into a dangerous shadowland. Galen prayed that the men who'd volunteered to stand guard over the tower would all be stationed within the old city. The Verrettis walked with their guns drawn, ready to shoot anyone who might look at them funny. Fortunately the park was empty of visitors at this hour, the guards all safely stationed on the far side, where any sane person would have expected the threat to originate.

High above, The Last Stronghold towered above them, its limestone walls pitted with age, one side gleaming silver in the moonlight, the other side in shadow. The Verrettis tugged them toward the shadowed side.

They worked silently, swiftly. Carlton pulled a wooden platform from its hiding place among the trees. With a heave, he set it in position straddling the rocky creek, giving them a stable place to stand.

Vincent pulled out a grappling hook launcher and aimed it carefully at the windows above. Propelled by compressed air, the hook shot upward in near silence. Galen and the others stayed well back in case the hook failed to catch. After Vincent tugged on the line several times, he seemed satisfied that the tines had achieved a sufficient hold.

As planned, Vince strapped himself into the harness, scooped up an armful of gear, then triggered the device's retractable mechanism. With his gun still trained on the figures below, he glided swiftly and silently upward into the dark night.

Galen stood below and prayed, ready, in spite of Milton's grasp on his arm and Carlton's gun at his back, to dart away with Ruby if he sensed an opening. But true to their plan, the bandits kept them covered as Vincent climbed through the window and disappeared.

They sent Ruby up next. Galen didn't like having her out of his sight, especially in those long moments when she was alone at the top of the tower with Vincent. Milton followed, leaving the youngest and burliest Verretti to make sure Galen didn't try anything—not that Galen would attempt to escape without Ruby.

By the time Galen rode to the top of the tower, Vincent had already torn open the panel on the floor. By climbing through the tower, they'd avoided many of the defense systems meant to protect the jewels. Galen glanced out the windows on the side facing the old city. The guards patrolled faithfully below, unaware that anything unusual was taking place above them.

Quickly, quietly, they hurried down the stairs and followed the short hallway to the blank stone wall, which Vince pulled open. He made eye contact with each of them in turn. They all knew they'd only have ten seconds to get inside. Vince had made it clear that, if either he or Ruby tried to separate themselves from the rest of the group, they'd be shot, no questions asked.

Not that he or Ruby had that chance. The Verrettis kept a tight grip on them every moment, guns drawn and ready.

Vince nodded to Ruby.

She stepped forward and placed her hand flat against the panel and entered the code.

The door slid open and green numbers counted down.

Galen had played through the next steps dozens of times in his mind, imagining how he'd thrust their captors aside, pull Ruby through to the safety of the vault and activate the quick lock that would close the doors behind them and raise the alarm at headquarters.

But the reality was nothing like his imagination. The Verrettis hardly gave them room to breathe, inserting their thick bodies between him and Ruby, their guns ready to fire reflexively if he or Ruby so much as twitched in the wrong direction.

They stepped through, and the Bulldog Bandits' eyes widened. The hardened jewel thieves, who had stolen more jewelry than he could even begin to imagine, looked impressed—even overwhelmed—by the jewels in the vault.

Ruby had tried the night before to explain to them that they wouldn't be able to take it all. They'd insisted otherwise, but now, as the vault doors slid shut automatically behind them, they hesitated.

"We can't take it all." Vincent spoke for the first time since they'd arrived.

The other two didn't argue.

"Let's get the best." Milton pointed to a Renaissance-era case, its opulent contents even more lavish than some of the others. The older Verretti looked at Galen expectantly.

Now it was his turn to betray the crown. Galen fought the urge to bolt. If he ran, they'd kill Ruby. If he cooperated, they'd steal the crown jewels.

In his heart of hearts, he'd hoped to have made his escape by now, to have Ruby safely tucked away where the Verrettis could never reach her. Even as he'd agreed to the Verrettis' plans the night before, he hadn't really believed it would come to this.

His fingers hesitated over the keypad.

A gun nudged hard under his ribs, and Ruby yelped.

Betray the crown? Or let them kill Ruby? They'd already come this far. Even if he resisted now, the Verrettis might try to smash and grab, or override the security devices themselves. He had to play along, but he didn't want to move too quickly.

From the moment Ruby had pressed her hand to the pad to open the door, the computer back at the royal guard headquarters had logged their entry. In light of the threat to the crown jewels, Selini had asked to have an alert message appear any time the computer logged entry at the vault.

Which meant the royal guards knew they were there, were probably contacting the guards patrolling outside at that very moment, asking them to find out what was up. But none of those guards had clearance to enter the passage to the vault.

No, the plan was to assemble in SWAT gear, to wait at the other end of the line and catch the thieves on their way out.

But the thieves wouldn't be going out past the guards. Galen's best hope was to stall, to make the bandits run late, in hopes that the swarming guards would encircle the tower completely, or Roxanne would arrive in time to attract attention. With all the guards on the old city side of the wall, they'd need time to reach the streets that passed through the old gates, a few blocks away on either side of where they were stationed.

Time. Galen would give them as much time as he could, but the only way to do that was to help the thieves. It would cost him his job. He had no doubt about that. But no matter how valuable the jewels inside the cases, they were just jewels. Ruby's life was worth more than that.

He pressed his thumb to the pad, entered the year of King Theodoric the Fourth's coronation, and watched as the hydraulic arms lifted the glass case silently away from the jewels.

Vincent grinned greedily as he let go of Ruby's arm and unfurled a collapsible padded bag, its interior a spider web of velvet compartments, and started transferring the priceless jewels inside.

Carlton motioned Galen over to the next case.

His stomach lurched no less as he cleared the thief to access that case. But even as he betrayed the crown he'd taken an oath to protect, he studied the bandits and the room around him, his thoughts spinning with possibilities.

The glass cases were bulletproof. If he and Ruby ducked behind one just as the door closed, the thieves would be stuck on the other side, unable to get back in. He'd have to trust the guards on the other side to capture the thieves. They'd risk letting the bandits get away with millions of dollars in jewels, but he might save Ruby.

But how would he get Ruby away from them? He'd been

considering that angle for the past thirty hours and had yet to find an opening.

Milton gestured to a case. Galen obediently opened it, thinking quickly.

The thieves would have their hands full with their bags. That would make them slower with their weapons, less able to keep a tight hold on him or on Ruby.

Galen's heart hammered inside him as he prayed for God to see them through, to show him an opening, to help him use it. He already knew the bandits were greedy. If he could use that greed against them, convince them to take more than they could easily carry, it would slow them down. It would give him a slight advantage.

He could see the readout on the large digital watch Milton wore, set to the fifteen-minute rendezvous agreement they'd made with Roxanne. They'd already been inside the vault for two minutes, with just over six minutes to go until they were to meet Roxanne on the ground.

Vincent selected his next case carefully. Already his sack bulged. Galen noticed the man hadn't asked either him or Ruby to carry a bag of jewels, though it would have greatly increased the amount they'd be able to steal. Why not? Did the bandits have no intention of letting them reach the SUV alive?

If that was the case, he and Ruby had just a few minutes left to live.

Galen opened the next case, counting down in his head. Vincent's sack would be full once he emptied this case. If the other two men each cleared out another case, they'd be ready to leave in a minute or so, just in time to meet with Roxanne when she circled back around.

As near as he could figure, Galen would cease to be useful to them once he opened the next two cases. At any point after that, they might decide to end his life. And they only needed Ruby's handprint to open the door. All they needed were the codes in his head, and then only for a few more seconds. After that, he and Ruby would no longer be necessary to their plans.

Milton took his time circling the cases, his greedy eyes bulging as he tried to choose what to leave and what to take.

Galen shuffled closer to Ruby. Vince had finally let go of her arm as he held his bag open with one arm and transferred jewels with the other. If Galen could get in between Ruby and the others, if he could maneuver her behind a case somehow, maybe he could figure out a way to hold her back when the door closed. The bandits had to leave the vault—with guards already likely swarming the tower, there was a chance they might be caught on their way out, if the guards could get to the other side of the wall in time.

The longer Galen could delay them, the better the odds were that the guards would catch them.

Ruby watched him approach, caution in her eyes. The bandits' attention was absorbed in their work. He took another step toward her.

"Hey—" Milton pointed his gun at Galen "—this one here." He gestured with the firearm.

Galen nodded and stepped toward him to open the case. "These pieces are all small. You could take more. What about this next case—would you like me to open it, as well?"

Milton raised his gun when Galen spoke—clearly the man didn't like anyone making suggestions. But then the elder Verretti looked at the jewels, and his greedy eyes widened.

Would he go for it? Galen prayed the man would get selfish. The more he had to carry, the slower he'd move.

But how much time did they need? Would the guards realize the bandits had come in from the other side of the wall? Or would they gain clearance to enter the passage and storm the vault, igniting a firefight that would leave everyone dead?

"Yeah, this case, too." Milton glanced at his watch as he scooped jewels into his bag. "But make it quick."

"You better hurry, Dad." Vincent closed his own bag,

grabbed Ruby by the arm, and pulled her toward the door. "Have him open it, then shoot him and let's get going."

Galen stepped toward the code panel on the second case. Would they shoot him the very second he opened it?

"Look, Vincent." Ruby pointed to another full case as Vincent tugged her toward the door. "Yellow diamonds. Your favorite. Galen can open this case for you, as well."

The bandits looked at each other as tense seconds crept by. Milton checked his watch. "You got time. Those are nice yellow diamonds."

"Open it," Vincent demanded.

Galen finished the code for the second case Milton had requested, then crossed the room toward where Vincent stood.

Vincent still had a tight hold on Ruby's arm. How would Galen get her away from the thief and behind the safety of the bulletproof cases?

"I want this case." Carlton gestured to a fourteenth century display dominated by sapphires.

"We need to get going." Milton tightened the drawstring on his bulging bag.

"It's only fair. You and Vince got three."

Galen hesitated, fingers above the panel for Vince's case. Once he entered the numbers, Vincent could shoot him just to keep his little brother from having his way—unless their father said otherwise.

"Hurry, then." Milton gestured with his gun.

Galen entered the numbers for Vince. As the lid rose upward on its hydraulic hinges, Galen pushed back on the case and felt it roll backward ever-so-slightly. The movement caught his attention, and he looked quickly at the other display cases in the room.

They were all on wheels.

The bulletproof lids they'd opened gaped upward still, providing a clear protective barrier. Galen had been trying to figure out how he could possibly get hold of Ruby and duck behind a case without getting shot. Impossible—he'd have to cross the room twice, surrounded by trigger-happy thieves. But if the cases moved, perhaps the task wouldn't be quite so impossible.

Thinking quickly, he crossed the room to Carlton. The cabinet he'd selected stood near the vault door between two open cases, their clear lids stretching upward, two feet high by three feet wide—big enough to hide behind if he was quick. While Carlton set his bag down, Galen grabbed the edge of the open case beside them.

Carlton pulled the drawstring open on his bag. Galen punched in the code.

Behind him, he heard Milton pull Ruby away from Vince. "Let's get this door open. Boys, you'll have ten seconds. Don't forget to clean up behind yourselves."

Galen understood the man's insinuation—he wanted his sons to shoot them in the vault. As the lid before him began to open, Carlton got his bag open, grabbed his gun and pointed it at Galen.

Quickly, deftly, Galen pulled the other wheeled case in front of him, stepping behind it and ducking low just as Carlton's first two shots hit the bulletproof glass, fracturing it into crystalline spiderwebs, but stopping the bullets from going through. Across the room, Ruby pressed her hand to the security panel.

As Galen propelled the case toward her on the smooth floor, the vault door slid open, the green numbers counting down.

Ruby had done her job.

Milton stepped through the door with his bulky bag over his shoulder.

Spinning around with the wheeled cabinet between him and the bandits, Galen grabbed Ruby and pulled her close to him, then backed quickly toward the line of cabinets on the other side of the room. Above them, the green light illuminated the numbers in sequence, counting down.

"Come on boys, we gotta go!" Milton called.

Carlton sent two more shots in their direction, missing the spinning case entirely as it settled to a stop in front of them. "Vincent!" He shouted at his brother.

Galen couldn't see past the case, but the numbers above them told him the brothers didn't have many seconds left.

"This way," Ruby tugged him toward the line of cases. Galen understood. With the glass already shattered, the case above them wouldn't remain bulletproof if it was hit again, especially at such close range. Still wearing his body armor, he covered her as best as he could as they ducked behind the row of cases.

Bullets hit the shattered glass behind them, sending it raining down in the spot where they'd been crouched a second before.

"Where'd they go? We can't leave them alive!" Carlton shouted from near the door.

"Carlton, we gotta go!" Vince's voice echoed from the chamber beyond the vault door as the numbers counted smoothly down. Three, two, one...

NINETEEN

Carlton sprayed a volley of bullets behind him and jumped through the doorway just as the one changed to zero.

Bullets hit the glass case, ricocheting off the walls even after the doors slid closed. Galen felt pain shoot through his shoulder, but he kept his head ducked low over Ruby and prayed. The explosive sound of bullets was followed by a tomblike silence.

Galen held tight to Ruby in the utter darkness of the sealed room. Pain speared through his back and arms as he listened closely, unsure whether any of the Verrettis had made it back through.

Silence. The family of thieves would be making their escape, racing against time to stay ahead of the guards who were surely swarming the tower on all sides by now.

"Are you okay?" Galen asked Ruby as he sucked in a breath.

She trembled beneath him. "I'm okay." Her small hands swept over his shoulders, across his back.

"Thank God. Ah." He winced as she brushed against a painful spot.

"They shot you," she whispered in the darkness. "You're bleeding."

"How bad?" The adrenaline that had kept him going eased from his system as he sagged to the floor. The room was completely dark. Should they try to exit? Not yet, not any time soon. He didn't want the Verrettis to hole up in the vault if the guards chased them back down the stairs.

"It's hard to tell in the dark." Her hands swept across his back again, gently, her touch soothing in spite of his pain. "Should I try to stop the bleeding, do you think? Or does that only make it worse?"

"Gentle pressure."

Ruby sniffled, and wetness splashed his face. Was she crying on him? Suddenly he wondered if she'd been hit after all. He wished he could see.

"Are you okay, Ruby? Are you injured?"

"I'm fine. But they got away with the jewels. And they shot you. Oh, Galen, I was so afraid of letting myself fall for you, afraid if you kissed me I wouldn't be able to leave Lydia." Her lips brushed his cheek, left a trail of kisses down the side of his face. "Don't leave me, Galen. Don't leave me."

He turned his head just far enough to kiss her full on the lips. His back protested the movement, but he didn't care.

Ruby returned the kiss, her gentle hands holding him in the cold darkness. "I've been so stupid. I thought if I didn't feel anything for you, it wouldn't hurt to leave. But what have I gained? Nothing. And I've wasted all the time we could have spent together."

"We can still spend time together."

Ruby found his hand and laced her fingers through his. "For a few weeks, maybe months, but I'll have to go home and fix my parents' stores. I should have taken advantage of the time we had together."

"I could leave with you."

She pulled away slightly. "What do you mean?"

"When you go back to the United States."

"But you could never leave the royal guard," Ruby protested softly. "Being a guard means everything to you."

"When I had to choose between protecting the crown jewels and protecting you, I realized what was most important. I'd give everything up to be with you. Besides, I won't be a guard after this."

"What?" She bent close to his face, her breath warm on his skin in the cold vault, her presence reassuring in the darkness.

"I helped the bandits steal the crown jewels. I'll be fired."

"You were shot. You did everything you could."

"It won't be enough. Captain Selini is already upset with me."

"You saved my life," Ruby whispered. "Won't that be enough?"

Galen doubted it would, not after the specific warnings the captain had given him. But he wasn't about to argue with her. She pressed her lips to his again, and he lost himself in her kiss, ignoring the pain and the cold of the floor, praying that somewhere above them the guards were arresting the Verrettis and bringing back the crown jewels.

"The princess calls you a hero, but the captain of the guard is mad at you."

Galen's brothers surrounded his hospital bed, plying him for more information. Galen didn't know much, only that the Verrettis had gotten away. The guards had thought to check the other side of the wall, but because of the roundabout route necessary to reach it, they'd arrived too late, the swiftest foot soldiers running up the path to the tower just as the boys piled into Roxanne's SUV, leaving their grappling hooks dangling from the tower as they pulled away.

The guards' earpiece radios had been jammed again, preventing clear communication and hampering their every effort. By the time they got a helicopter over the spot, there was no sign of the SUV.

Officially, the palace had not disclosed what the thieves had taken, only that items of value had been stolen and the royal guard would be following several leads. Pictures of the Verrettis were being circulated throughout Lydia and the surrounding region. And Galen had yet to be fired.

"What did they get away with?" Adrian asked, who had friends in the guard. All Galen's brothers were career army men. Four years of service in the Lydian army was a prerequisite for being a guard. Galen's brothers had gone through basic training with many of his fellow guards. The guards wouldn't share classified information.

Clearly, his brothers didn't like being kept in the dark.

Galen didn't like it, either. He wanted to be out of bed and back at headquarters. Linus had come by—mostly to learn how badly he'd been injured—and had briefed him on the bare essentials. It wasn't enough. Galen needed to know if they had any idea which direction the Verrettis had gone, if they'd found the boat, if the guards had talked to Rocco, if Ruby was okay.

Ruby.

Had she been injured? She'd told him she was fine, but it had been dark in the vault, and once Kirk had rushed in with the guards at his heels, everything had been chaotic. As one of the few with high-level clearance, Kirk had led a team in SWAT gear through the long way. They'd been inside the wall when the bandits had escaped, and had missed them completely.

The guards had escorted Ruby out first, forcing Galen to lie still until they determined he could walk out, injured though he was. He'd been trying to describe the SUV, shouting at them to check the place where the boat had been docked, insisting they leave him and head after the bandits. Kirk thought the other guards would be after the getaway vehicle by then. But they couldn't communicate because their earpieces had been jammed and there wasn't a phone signal in the vault.

The Bulldog Bandits had gotten away.

In his hospital bed, Galen tried to sit up. He needed to get to headquarters, needed to share everything he knew.

"Whoa there." Timothy, his middle brother, nearly tackled him flat on the bed. "You're not going anywhere. You still have an IV in your arm. You haven't been discharged yet."

Galen followed the line from his hand to the dripping machine. He couldn't imagine why he still needed it. Granted, the bullet that had ricocheted off the vault wall had grazed his shoulder, scraping away a wide swath of skin, causing him to lose a great deal of blood. He was supposed to have his bandages changed periodically as the doctor was afraid of an infection.

But the Bulldog Bandits had the crown jewels. Galen couldn't just stay in bed.

"If you guys are going to hang around anyway, sign the papers to get me out of here." Galen ripped the tape away from the IV, pulled the needle carefully from his vein and applied pressure to keep it from bleeding. "I've got places to go."

"Dressed like that?" Milos, the oldest, laughed at Galen's hospital gown.

"I've got clothes around here somewhere." He found them in the wardrobe cupboard and pulled on his pants.

Timothy held up Galen's blood-splattered shirt. "You're not wearing this." Sunlight from the window highlighted the bloodstain and the gaping bullet hole.

Pain shot through Galen's back as he straightened and zipped his pants. He looked at his brothers. Timothy wore a polo over a T-shirt. All the brothers were nearly the same size.

"Tim, give me your shirt."

The brothers teased him about taking the shirts off their backs, but they helped Galen pull the polo on when he discovered he could hardly raise his arms above his head.

"You're seriously busting out of the hospital?" Milos looked at him like he was crazy, but there was something in his voice that edged on respect.

"I've got things to do. In case you hadn't guessed it, something big is going on. I'm not going to lie here while—" Galen caught himself, while his brothers looked at him expectantly hoping for intel. "While something big goes on."

Milos nodded. "I'll sign you out of here and find out if that IV was important."

"You'll need a car." Adrian pulled out his keys. "I'll drive."

"I need to get a fresh shirt." Timothy followed them into the hall. "I don't want to miss this."

Captain Selini saw Galen privately in his office. "We found the boat on the dock where you said it would be. It was swept clean, no personal effects, no fingerprints, nothing but a few stray bulldog hairs."

"Rocco might know—"

"Rocco's phone goes straight to voice mail, ditto the phone number we have for the Verrettis. We tried to call and get a ping-back from the towers, but they won't pick up, so we can't trace their signal. We've tried everything, but we've got nothing."

"So we have no idea where they are?"

"We know a few things. We don't believe they've left Lydia. We put up checkpoints on all the roads leading out of the country. They couldn't possibly have made it to any of the borders before that. And we're checking all commercial flights out of Lydia."

"What about private planes?" Galen knew the Verrettis could afford their own jet or helicopter.

"None that have taken off from registered airfields, and there have been no reports of any unregistered flight activity—just the military and guard helicopters that were sent out to look for them."

"And by sea?"

"That's our weakest point. We checked all boats at the marina, but given Lydia's rugged coastline and the archipelago, watercraft could be hiding anywhere. We're searching from the air, but so far, nothing."

Nothing. The word echoed in Galen's thoughts. "We've got nothing else to go on? No other possible leads?"

The captain looked at him evenly, his face tired, even haggard in spite of his relative youth. Jason Selini seemed to be weighing something, debating a decision he didn't want to make. Finally he leaned forward, his voice low, as though he feared the walls themselves might hear. "Princess Anastasia ordered tracking devices."

Galen's heart beat so loudly he could hardly hear the captain over the pounding in his ears. The princess had talked about ordering such devices, but had said they would take a while to arrive, and with her busy schedule in preparation for the wedding...

"The devices arrived via airmail the morning after you and Ruby were kidnapped. The princess insisted on installing them immediately, but..."

"But?"

"We tried to test their range and precision. The devices registered when she brought them over to headquarters and we installed the software. We followed their trail all the way to the old city walls and up the tower. And then..."

"Then?" Galen could guess, but he needed to know for certain.

"We lost them. It seems the vault is too far underground, the stones too thick for the transmitters' signals to penetrate."

"But the bandits carried the jewels back out."

"We picked up the signal as soon as they did, just as the guards called in to tell us the bandits had escaped on the other side of the wall. It was chaos here last night." The captain turned to the monitor beside him, angled it so Galen could see.

"So where—?"

"This is where we lost them again. Labyrinth Caves National Park."

Galen swallowed, defeat clawing at his heart through the pain in his back.

The Labyrinth Caves were a national treasure, boasting over one hundred miles of explored passageways, in addition to untold miles of spurs that had never been documented, running in a tangled maze beneath the Lydian mountains southeast of Sardis. Though the main entrances were regulated, dozens of peephole entries dotted the park, to the delight of spelunkers who traveled to Lydia just to explore the tangled underground network. But occasionally, spelunkers got lost inside. Search parties would comb the caves for days to find them—and those were people who wanted to be found.

If the bandits wanted to remain hidden, they could hide inside the caves forever, the thick limestone blocking any signal the tracking devices might try to send.

"What about their SUV?"

"It's not there. We suspect the driver left part of their party with the jewels, then drove away, probably to coordinate the next step in their escape."

Galen closed his eyes. Pain radiated through him, pounding its message home. It was over. The bandits had won. They were going to get away with everything—had all but gotten away with it already.

"But if they come out with the jewels, the tracking devices will pick up their trail again." He grasped at fading hope.

"Assuming the bandits don't discover and disable the devices first. These are trained gemologists we're dealing with."

Galen hung his head. It *was* over. They'd gotten away.

Jason Selini cleared his throat. "I'm going to see through the security in place for Isabelle's wedding. I'll stay on long enough for the new recruits to transition from the Lydian army."

"Sir?" Galen prompted when his captain fell silent.

"The crown jewels were stolen on my watch." The captain met his eyes, sadness brimming in their steel-gray depths. "If they're not recovered, I will resign."

TWENTY

"Galen!" Ruby nearly jumped as the guard burst into the palace suite that served in place of Princess Stasi's studio. "They told me you wouldn't be released from the hospital for days."

"It's a hospital, not a prison. They can't keep me there." He strode toward her, wincing when she placed a hand on his arm.

She pulled her hand away. "Where can I touch you that won't hurt?"

Thick bandages padded his shoulder, but the pain on his face gave way to a smile. "On my lips."

She kissed him as gently as she could, tempted to lose herself in the kiss, but too many questions still hadn't been answered. She pulled away reluctantly. "Did they let you keep your job?"

"The captain didn't mention it. He said something even worse."

"What could be worse?"

"He said he'll step down if the jewels aren't recovered." Galen lowered himself into the nearest chair.

"How is that worse?"

"Ever since the attacks, the royal guard's image has been tarnished. We've been trying to restore the honor of the guard. We've weeded out anyone with ties to the insurgents, we've been working double shifts to make up for the men we lost, waiting for the army to clear men for transfer, men with no treasonous connections. And now that we're on the brink of finally having a full staff, of being in a position to be effective again, he's going to quit. Even if I keep my job, what good will it do? The guard can't afford another setback, not after all we've lost."

Ruby felt his sorrow deep inside her. Galen loved being a guard, loved Lydia and the royal family, loved guarding all those he held dear. She hated to see him lose that, to lose even the chance to work toward restoring what had been damaged. She felt it with the same desperate determination that had coursed through her the night before when she'd feared Galen might die in her arms.

Somehow they had to fix things.

"We'll find them. We'll recover the jewels—then the captain won't have to step down."

"I'd love to do that, Ruby, but how?"

"Stasi got the tracking devices implanted. She ordered two dozen devices. Fourteen of them are in jewels still in the vault. The other ten are with the bandits."

"Ten of them?" Galen sounded as though she'd shared bad news. "How can that many devices escape their notice? If they find one, they'll tear everything apart until they find the rest."

"Stasi knew what she was doing. She hid them well. She's a trained gemologist."

"So are the Verrettis."

Ruby had to admit his words were true, but she wasn't about to give up hope. "They won't tear apart the jewels and risk destroying their value in the process." She looked at him, pleading silently that he wouldn't take away her last shred of hope.

"Ruby," he said her name softly, reaching for her, wincing as he stretched out his arm.

She kissed him again, loving it, loving him, but at the same time wondering if she wasn't just causing herself more pain in the long run. She still had to return to the U.S. and fix her parents' business—much more urgently now that she'd found out what the Verrettis had done to sabotage it. Given Galen's devotion to the guard, she knew she couldn't ask him to come with her. Granted, he'd offered to follow her, but she knew his heart was in Lydia. It would tear him apart to move.

She couldn't ask him to make that sacrifice.

The door burst open with a loud bang and three men poured through, talking at once.

"There he is."

"Now we know why he was in such a hurry to leave the hospital."

A charming fellow in a T-shirt extended his hand toward her. "I don't believe we've been introduced."

"These are my brothers," Galen explained hastily, "Milos, Timothy and Adrian. Guys, this is Ruby Tate, assistant to Princess Anastasia."

"A pleasure." Timothy shook her hand.

Milos shook a bottle at Galen. "That IV you pulled out was your pain medicine. Take one of these or you'll be crying for Mom within the hour."

Galen held out one hand. Milos handed over a pill, which Galen swallowed. "What are you guys doing here, anyway? You don't have clearance to be inside the palace."

"We're here to help."

"Show him the badges."

"It was supposed to be a surprise." The brothers jostled each other as they held out their wallets for Galen to see.

"We're transferring from the army," Milos explained with a broad smile.

"To the guard? But you guys always said—"

"Somebody's got to keep an eye on you."

"Mom worries about you."

"But—" Adrian held out a hand, silencing the others "—we

don't officially start until next week, so if you want our help, you're going to have to tell us what's going on."

Ruby had been desperate to hear what the guard knew, and felt grateful that Galen didn't ask her to leave as he explained all he'd learned.

"So they're in the caves?" Timothy clarified as Galen finished his explanation.

"Yes, unless the bandits have found all ten tracking devices and destroyed them. But I doubt they'd have stashed the jewels and left. Most likely they're guarding them, armed to the teeth, ready to hide if they hear someone coming and shoot if anyone gets too close." Galen started to shake his head, winced, froze. "I don't want you going in there."

"How else are we supposed to flush them out?" Milos asked.

"I'm familiar with the caves," Timothy added. "In fact, I can think of several likely spots where they might be hiding."

"And with Isabelle's wedding rehearsal today and the ceremony tomorrow, your captain can't spare a single man on such a long-shot mission. We're perfect for the job."

Ruby felt her hopes, which had been nearly crushed, rise again with new life. But Galen looked terrified at the thought of letting his brothers walk willingly into danger.

"Mom will never forgive me if anything happens to any of you." Galen's face had gone white, either from overexerting himself too soon after his injury, or out of fear for his brothers, or both. "I regret that I've told you as much as I have."

"Nothing's going to happen to us. We're professionals." The brothers waved off his concerns and headed for the door, conferring about helmets and armor and weapons.

Galen rose unsteadily to his feet. "I've got to stop them. They'll get themselves killed."

"No." Ruby waved him back down, afraid to touch him for fear of upsetting his injury. "You need to take it easy. Rest. Isabelle's wedding is tomorrow. I've been invited to attend."

"It's a public event. You'll need a guard." Galen frowned, probably wondering who the royal guard could possibly spare.

"Precisely." She smiled at him. "You'll need to rest if you're going to accompany me."

Galen checked his phone discreetly below the edge of the banquet table. Still no word on anything. His brothers had last checked in hours ago, not long before the wedding started, to let him know they hadn't found the bandits yet.

Not even the beautiful wedding reception could ease the ominous feeling in Galen's gut. The wedding had gone off perfectly, a blur of flowers and music. Or perhaps they'd only seemed that way to Galen, who'd kept his eyes mostly on Ruby throughout it all.

"Is everything okay?" Ruby leaned close, her red hair a marvel of curls and jeweled clips, her curves draped in a turquoise dress which made her eyes look even more dazzling than usual.

He stared at her for just a moment, memorizing her every feature. She'd be going back to the U.S. far too soon. He didn't ever want to forget her beauty.

"Galen?" Her prompt carried concern.

"No word," Galen assured her. "But I can't shake this feeling—"

"Your brothers will be fine. They're big boys." She clearly wanted to make him smile.

He wished he could smile, but anxiety ate at him. "The Verrettis aren't stupid. They know we're watching them, that the roads still have checkpoints, that the airport security is on high alert, looking for them. Unless they want to hide in those caves forever, they've got to know tonight is their best shot at escaping, while everyone's distracted with the wedding."

"Simon and Oliver are both on duty tonight," Ruby reminded him. "If those tracking devices move, they'll call."

"They'll call Selini first." Galen watched as the captain

circled the room, alert, watching the dancing begin, keeping a wide distance between himself and the wedding planner.

Galen looked back down at his phone.

Still nothing.

He wiggled his earpiece, which the guards had switched to a different frequency. They were careful not to reveal anything sensitive when they used the devices, but they weren't able to do away with their use altogether, not when they had such a large gathering to coordinate. He shifted uncomfortably in his seat, his back angry about his prolonged seated position.

"Dance with me?" Ruby slipped her hand into his.

Galen swallowed. His back might appreciate the change of position, but he'd only make things worse. "The captain will see."

"Is that a problem?"

With regret, Galen realized he'd never explained the captain's injunction. "Captain Selini warned me not to get involved with you."

"What? Why? Other guards—"

"It's because of the other guards. He doesn't want the royal guard to form a reputation. He's not happy about the others but they're seeing royalty, so what can he do?"

"Will he fire you?" Ruby asked. "Don't dance with me, then. I don't want to cause trouble."

Galen thought about it a moment longer, his mind feeling sluggish and disoriented from the pain in his back and the pills that dulled it. It didn't matter if Selini fired him, really. Ruby wanted to dance. And Galen wanted to dance with her.

He stood and extended his hand. "They're starting another slow song."

"I thought—" She rose halfway, then started to sit again. "Your job—"

"You matter more to me than my job." He raised his most imploring eyebrow. "Dance with me?"

They made it halfway to the dance floor, Galen's back sending warning shots through his spine, making him question the wisdom of moving, when Ruby stopped.

"Selini's on the phone," she whispered.

Galen turned discreetly to the spot where he'd last seen his captain. At the sight of Selini's face, he changed direction.

Jason Selini looked up, a ripple of relief passing over his face when he spotted them approaching. He strode to meet them. "They've jammed our radio frequency again, but Oliver just called—he's picked up the signal from the tracking devices. They're out of the caves headed toward the north exit of the park."

"I'll go."

Concern and apology mingled on Selini's face. "I'm calling Sam and Paul. I don't know who else we can spare."

"Keep the wedding guests safe. We'll handle it." Galen ignored the shooting pain as he darted from the banquet hall, punching a call to his brothers, then ran down the back stairs toward the garage, into the darkness of the mild September evening.

Milos didn't answer.

Timothy didn't answer.

Galen wondered if they were still deep in the cave, too far below ground for their phones to pick up his call. He reached the garage, smashed his thumb against the print pad on the cabinet that held the vehicle keys, and pulled out the set to a jeep as he sent a call to Adrian.

"I'm coming with you." Ruby nearly blocked his way.

"You can't. It's far too dangerous." He prayed his brother would answer the phone.

"You're supposed to be guarding me."

"Only if you leave the safety of the palace grounds." He moved past her to the jeep. "Go to headquarters. See if Oliver and Simon need your help—you'll be safest there."

"Yeah?" Adrian answered the phone in a breathless voice

as Galen climbed into the vehicle, his body protesting his every movement.

"The jewels are moving toward the north park exit."

"No kidding." Adrian panted. He sounded like he was running hard. "Thanks for the phone calls, bro, you gave me the moment of distraction I needed."

"What do you mean?" Galen clicked the garage door open and got the jeep started and shoved into gear, trying to listen and shift at the same time.

"The Verrettis have Milos and Timothy. They had me, too, until two minutes ago."

"What?" Galen nearly shouted as he paused at the back gate, waiting impatiently for Elias to make it open while Sam ran past him toward the garage.

"They took us hostage as an insurance plan in case they encounter any trouble on their way out of town."

"Then what are they going to do with them?" Galen tried to steer, to think.

"According to their threats, once they've served their purpose, the bandits plan to dump their bodies at sea."

TWENTY-ONE

Ruby looked at the thumb pad on the key cabinet across the room, thinking quickly. Her handprint had opened the underground vault. And she'd been authorized to use vehicles during her stay—had even driven a few, but only after someone had handed her the keys. Would her thumbprint work on the box?

Sam had nearly seen her when he'd run in, grabbed some keys, hopped on a motorcycle and gone zipping off. Paul darted in next. Ruby hid in the shadows and picked out a vehicle while Paul grabbed another jeep. The moment he pulled out of the garage, she hoisted her skirts and leaped toward the key cabinet. If she didn't hurry, she wouldn't be able to follow them.

She pressed her thumb to the pad and prayed.

A light turned green.

Ruby quickly found the keys she wanted hanging on an American fob. They went to the eco-friendly green Chevy Spark she'd driven a few times before they'd assigned her a guard. It wasn't powerful, but it was familiar, and considering that she had no idea what she was getting into, she needed a vehicle she was accustomed to.

She dived in, pulling on her seat belt as she started the car, catching up to Paul and leaving the palace grounds before the gate closed after him, praying that in the darkness and confusion, no one would bother to stop her.

No one did.

Paul took a few corners quickly and Ruby did the same, praying for everyone's safety, praying they'd recover the crown jewels. And what had Galen learned from his phone call to his brother? Something that had turned his face pale. Whatever it was, she prayed God would work that out, too.

Paul reached the arterial highway that cut through town and turned south.

Toward the caves.

But Ruby wondered if the Verrettis would still be there. Oliver had picked up the signal and called Selini, who'd talked to Galen, who'd run for the garage. Ruby had stayed out of sight, taken the car, followed Paul…it all took time. How much time? Enough that the Verrettis should be far from the park.

Her headlights illumined the inside of Paul's car in front of her. She could see the outline of his hand holding a phone to his ear, watched him slow, wait for an oncoming vehicle to pass and then whip around in a one-eighty, heading north again.

Ruby slowed, waiting for cars to pass, praying for a break so she could follow Paul. Finally, thanking God for the Spark's tight turning radius, she flipped a U-turn behind him and accelerated, desperate to find the vehicle she'd been following, as that was her only link to the trail.

More cars poured onto the highway as Ruby approached an on-ramp. She couldn't see Paul's car, couldn't see anything but a sea of red taillights blurring in the darkness.

What now? Where should she go?

The Verrettis could be headed anywhere, but if they wanted to get out of Lydia, they'd most likely head for the airport or the marina. And given the level of security at the Sardis International Airport, Ruby guessed they'd make for the sea.

Lydia's jagged coastline jutted out from Sardis at odd angles, the irregular lines exacerbated by the hills of the city. Ruby knew of at least three main roads that led to different parts of the marina. Which one should she take?

She topped a hill, paused for a stop sign, thought quickly. She didn't know which road to take, wasn't even sure she knew how to find her way through the tangled, narrow streets. There was a road that led downhill from the palace to the north end of the marina. She could find that one. It might be the least direct route, but at least she wouldn't run the risk of getting lost and wasting more time.

Ruby steered the Spark north, praying the others were having more success at tracking down the bandits.

Galen stopped by the side of the road, his phone tight to his ear. "Do you see my headlights?" He checked the mile marker Adrian had named. He was in the right spot. Where was Adrian?

A heavily armored figure burst through the bushes helmet first and dived for the jeep.

"We've got to hurry." Galen threw the vehicle in Reverse as his brother climbed in. "You're sure you can recognize their vehicle?"

"Conversion van. Black. No plates. Let's go." Adrian drummed the dashboard impatiently.

Galen accelerated, hoping he'd made the right decision in taking the time to pick up his brother. The Verrettis could be anywhere by now—but only Adrian knew what they were driving. It was an advantage Galen needed, possibly his only advantage, since they'd tried switching to alternate radio frequencies only to find those jammed, as well. Not that he was terribly surprised. The bandits knew what they were doing.

He tossed his phone to his brother. "Call the last number dialed," he instructed him. "Ask Oliver to set up a conference call. I have to drive."

As they neared the city, Galen could see that traffic was

thick. Of course, with Isabelle's wedding that day, most of Lydia had swarmed the city to watch the wedding procession as it traveled from the cathedral to the palace for the reception. "It's going to take forever to get to the marina."

"Take the bypass. The exit's right up here."

Unsure whether Adrian had inside information from the phone, or if he was simply trying to avoid the congestion of the city, Galen took the exit. "Where are the Verrettis?"

"They've almost reached the marina."

"Already?"

"Selini got the army to dispatch helicopters. It's okay. We're going to stay on top of them."

Ruby was almost to the marina when a black van cut her off, forcing her to slam on her brakes and swerve to avoid hitting them. She recovered quickly, straightening the vehicle and continuing behind them.

Above, she heard helicopters swarming the air. Two? No, three.

The van in front of her slammed on the brakes and started backing up. Glad she'd opted for a familiar vehicle, Ruby threw the Spark in Reverse just in time to avoid being hit—again. She backed around a parked car and watched as the van pulled past her, the occupants gawking at the sky.

Recognition hit her full force.

The Verrettis.

Ruby ducked. Had they seen her? With her red hair she was instantly recognizable. When she peered up over the steering wheel again, half expecting to see Vince with a gun at her window, the van had turned and was headed down a concrete pier.

They were getting away!

Leaving the Spark, Ruby darted behind a truck and peered around. The Verrettis stopped their van at the end of the pier where a sleek motorboat waited. Darkness had fallen, but one of the circling helicopters shined a high-powered beam of light at the craft, enough for Ruby to make out Roxanne at the helm, gunning the engines as Milton and the boys leaped from the van in a jumble of bags and legs—too many legs for just three people.

Ruby recognized them with a sinking heart, about the same moment as the men in the open doorways of the helicopters above aimed their weapons but held their fire. The Verrettis had Milos and Timothy, using them as human shields to keep the gunmen above from firing. Roxanne threw the boat in gear and pulled away from the dock as the men jumped aboard.

Now what? The Verrettis were getting away with the crown jewels of Lydia and two of Galen's brothers—who, Ruby was sure, they'd do away with once they'd served their purpose. Most of the boat traffic in the marina had come in to dock when the helicopters had showed up, but Ruby saw two royal guard jet skis shoot away from the south end of the marina. Paul and Sam? In the darkness she couldn't be certain.

But one thing was perfectly clear. The Verrettis had no intention of stopping in spite of the helicopters that circled above them. And what were two jet skis against such a powerful speedboat? Even if they caught up to the craft and positioned themselves directly in front of it, the Verrettis would plow through them without blinking.

The guards needed a bigger boat. Something equally as powerful as the Verrettis' boat, and equally as fast. Ruby recalled the boat Galen had borrowed from the royal guard two summers before when he'd taken her and Stasi out to view the falling stars. That boat was docked at the pier, bobbing at the moorings next to a thumbprint reader.

Would hers work on that thumb pad, too? Ruby didn't hesitate. She drew up the flowing skirt of her gown so she could run unhindered down the dock, glad she'd opted for ballet flats instead of impractical heels. She reached the mooring and mashed her thumb against the print pad, praying for recognition and clearance as the thick weatherproof coating slowed the device's response.

Green light.

She opened the lid, unhooked the cable that held the boat in place, grabbed the keys and hitched up her skirt a little higher as she climbed aboard, praying fervently, inaudibly, that God would keep her safe, protect Galen's brothers, and bring the Bulldog Bandits to justice. Somehow.

The panel of instruments at the helm wasn't the same as what Ruby remembered from two summers before. It wasn't the same boat, she realized. That boat had malfunctioned and apparently had been replaced. Ruby found the keyhole, found the one that fit it, stared at the throttle and tried to remember what Galen had said as he'd explained how to start the boat. Was it prime the throttle or disengage the engine? And something about a bilge…something?

She realized she'd been too focused on the charming bend of Galen's eyebrows to listen actively to his words. Far in the distance now, the Verrettis sped through a gap between islands, helicopters swarming like seagulls, persistent in their pursuit but unwilling to strike.

"Throttle." She placed her hand on the control piece, unsure whether she was supposed to push it now or after she'd turned the key. "Bilge…bilge…something." She looked around frantically, wishing the instruments were labeled.

"Blower." A deep voice spoke in her ear. Hands came round her on either side, familiar fingers cupped hers as they pushed the throttle forward. "You were supposed to stay at the palace."

"Galen." Ruby would have hugged him, but he had his hands full operating the controls. "And…Adrian?" She wasn't completely certain which brother had joined them.

"Thanks for getting her unhooked." Adrian nodded. "Saved us a step. We have to hurry. You need to get down and stay down. And find yourself a life vest. Things could get rough."

Life vests weren't difficult to find. Ruby strapped one on as instructed, not wanting to hinder their efforts in the slightest. Considering the bandits had Galen's brothers, not even the crown jewels themselves seemed so important. There were lives at stake—Galen's brothers' lives. Why had they thought the jewels were so important that they'd willingly risked their lives?

The boat leaped faster over the waves created by the Verrettis' wake, becoming airborne as it hurtled from breaker to breaker, slamming with jaw-jarring madness every time it smacked down. Finally Galen pulled close enough to steer smoothly through the channel the bandits' boat had cut through the warm waters, and Ruby took advantage of the relative stillness to shuffle forward, gripping the grab rail, as she moved toward Galen and his brother, two life vests tucked under her arm. Both men, she could see, wore body armor, which would only weigh them down if they ended up in the water.

She shoved a vest at Adrian, who gave her half a smile and strapped it on.

Galen took one look at the vest and cringed. Given his injuries, putting on the vest would be a painful process. She shoved it over his head anyway, reached around him to clip the strap securely across his chest.

"What can I do to help?" She had to shout to be heard over the roar of the helicopters and the screaming engine of the boat.

"Get down!" Galen had submitted to the vest without fighting her, but he looked terrified at the thought of having her in the open next to him. "I have to get in front of them if I'm going to get them to stop!"

Ruby shuffled backward then, ducking low. She'd heard the snipers in the open bays of the helicopters sending precise volleys of bullets spraying across the Verrettis' boat, probably aiming for the engine or the gas tank, but either the boat was made of bulletproof materials or their targets were somewhere beneath the hostages, because the bandits hadn't even slowed down.

She stayed down, near the back of the boat where she'd be out of Galen and Adrian's way, where the spray that splashed past the windshield doused her unabatedly, drenching her hair and her gown, chilling her with the cool night air that streamed against her arms and tore the pins from her hair.

Galen had steered free of the Verrettis' wake channel. When Ruby peeked up over the side, she saw they'd pulled nearly even with the speedboat, its streamlined surface projecting forward with a long hull, the rear seating area inadequate for the six large figures in the back.

Beyond them Ruby spotted the royal guard jet skis, barely keeping up in spite of the bandits' zigzagging evasive maneuvers, falling farther behind as the Verrettis increased their speed. When the racing boat swerved their way, Ruby saw Adrian perched on the gunwale, holding the wet guardrail with one hand as he extended his other arm for balance.

"A little closer, bro!"

The Verrettis didn't seem to hear him. Roxanne was focused on steering through the maze of islands that loomed in the darkness ahead. Milton had his gun out, shooting at the helicopters that taunted them from above. Carlton and Vince struggled to keep their feet while training their guns on Milos and Timothy. Somewhere, probably under a seat or secure in a storage compartment, they'd tucked away the crown jewels, out of sight.

Galen looked, swerved until Ruby feared they'd ram the Verrettis' boat, and corrected the other direction as Adrian lunged at Carlton, nearly missing the boat entirely but grabbing the bandit's gun arm, knocking the weapon into the water as he swung his legs around and propelled himself into the crowded seats.

Vince spun toward him, gun first, and Ruby ducked, aware she was in the line of fire and still close to the other boat, though Galen had swerved away, gunning the engine to faster speeds, chopping through the copter-stirred waters.

When Ruby peeked over the gunwale again, she saw chaos on the other boat. Adrian had somehow disarmed Carlton and Vince, and though Milton waved his gun and cursed at them, between the bouncing boat and the tangle of Harris brothers, Milton didn't dare shoot—not without risking hitting one of his own sons.

Adrian seemed to have an advantage, but Milos and Timothy were both handcuffed and therefore unable to help much, besides a few well-placed elbow jabs. One of the bulldogs had climbed up on a seat and barked furiously at the scuffling men. Ruby wished she could think of some way to help them. She looked around the boat, lifting the seats and ruffling through the dark storage compartments, finding little more than life preservers and blankets inside.

Her fingers hit something hard.

A fire extinguisher? Why not? Galen was slowly gaining on the distracted bandits. When he swerved close again, this time nearly clipping the bow, Ruby pulled the clip from the fire extinguisher, pointed the nozzle toward Roxanne and pulled the trigger.

A white cloud shot through the air, agitated by the copters above them, painting Milton's back and Roxanne's face with its spray.

Roxanne swiped at her face with one hand but pushed the throttled relentlessly forward as the boat sped through the cloud, enveloping the men at the rear, before the swerving boats veered apart, too far for the spray to reach.

Vince cursed and grabbed Milos. As Ruby watched, horrified, he shoved the handcuffed man over the rail into the open water.

Adrian shouted as his brother went under, unable to swim with his hands bound. Instantly, almost reflexively, Ruby grabbed the life preserver and threw it with all her might, but between her bulky life vest and the blasting wind off the boats, she couldn't throw it far. It tumbled through the air, a circle of white against the dark sea, and hit the water far from where Milos had gone in.

Carlton laughed before turning on Timothy. Adrian got between them at the last second, but Vincent had his hands free again and helped shove the other brother overboard.

Hesitation flashed across Adrian's face for only a second before he dived after his brothers.

Ruby grabbed the rail, unsure if she'd be of any assistance to them in her flowing gown. She could no longer see where Milos had gone in. How could she ever reach him in the darkness?

The distant drone of the jet skis changed pitch as the guards slowed the nimble crafts. They'd been falling progressively farther behind, the recreational vehicles simply not powerful enough to keep up with the speed boat. The guards circled round to where Milos and Timothy had gone in.

Ruby breathed a sigh of relief. Sam and Paul had gone back for the brothers.

The high-powered beam from a helicopter swept across the waves, illuminating the rescue behind them even as the boats sped forward, leaving the men behind.

"Now what?" Ruby screamed as she inched across the slippery deck toward Galen.

He grimaced, his face tight with pain as he fought to push the jarring boat to greater speeds. "I've got to cut them off. There's a strip of underwater sandbars near the long island ahead. The tide is low. There's a chance, if I can steer them that way, we could ground them on the sandbars."

"Good plan. What can I do?"

"Distract them. If they see the sandbars, they'll steer away. We're almost past the islands now. Once they reach open water, they'll be out of our jurisdiction."

"I'll look for another fire extinguisher." The one she'd used was nearly empty.

"Good idea." Galen swerved closer to the speedboat again.

"Anything else I can do?" She fought to control her shivering as the change in the boat's trajectory blasted her with a fresh gust of cold wind.

"Pray."

Ruby prayed hard and found one more fire extinguisher, then watched and waited for the right moment to use it. It was the last weapon she had. She couldn't waste it.

TWENTY-TWO

Galen steered directly toward the nose of the Verrettis' boat. They were coming up on the sandbars far too quickly, and unless they turned hard, they'd miss the sandbars completely.

And then what? Grateful as he was that Paul and Sam had stopped to pluck his brothers from the sea, it left him essentially alone against the speedboat. The helicopters had tried firing now that his brothers were no longer in the way, but with their chopping blades cutting through the dark sky, the pilots had to focus on staying clear of each other. They had yet to get close enough to the bandits' boat to do any real damage.

A new sound echoed through the night, higher pitched than the roaring all around him. Galen ignored the pain that shot through him with every movement and turned to see what had made the sound.

Another boat, a black cigarette boat, faster and sleeker than even the Verrettis' craft, steered toward them from the cover of the north end of the island.

Who? What? An accomplice, coming to meet the bandits and help them get away?

Whoever it was, Galen didn't care. Given the boat's angle of approach, the Verrettis had no choice but to steer closer to the island.

And the sandbars.

Galen bore down on them, increasing his speed in one

last desperate attempt to get ahead of them and cut them off. Roxanne had slowed ever-so-slightly when she'd spotted the cigarette boat approaching.

Why? Because she was planning to come alongside them and board? Or because the other boat bore down on them as though unafraid of the island or any other threat that might lay hidden below the low tide waters?

"I've got one fire extinguisher," Ruby had crept forward again and stood near his ear to talk without shouting. "Tell me when you want me to use it."

Still unsure what the cig boat was doing or whether he ought to fear the black craft, Galen gunned hard, straightening only slightly as he prepared for an abrupt swerve.

"Ready. Aim." Pale shadows stretched like fingers just beneath the waves ahead.

Vincent saw, pointed, opened his mouth to warn his mother.

"Fire." Galen swerved at the bandits.

White spray caught Vince full in the face, choking him, blinding Roxanne from seeing the sandbar. The speedboat plowed toward the strip of sand.

Galen eased away, pulling ahead of the bandits as the disoriented driver slowed the boat.

The Verrettis hit the first sandbar head-on, bouncing high, slamming down, curses and the barking of bulldogs filling the night air as Ruby's fire extinguisher spent its spray.

"Sandbar!" Vincent screamed between curses.

Roxanne jerked the wheel toward Galen. The boat tore through the water, hitting the next sandbar at an angle, launching sideways through the air.

Galen turned the wheel to the side as the airborne boat sailed toward them almost on its side now. "Ruby, watch out!"

Behind him, Ruby scrambled across the slippery deck to starboard as the Verrettis' speedboat shot toward them, careening sideways, then slammed into the side of the royal guard boat.

The body armor on Galen's chest hit the steering wheel, knocking the breath from his lungs, the pain so intense it shot across his field of vision as a white streak of light. He raised his head slowly, blinking, losing speed as the wounded boat took on water.

"Ruby!" He gasped as soon as his lungs found air.

"Here. I'm here." Her hands swept down his arm, her fingers linking with his, cold as the night air, trembling.

Galen raised his head, the pain too fierce to allow him to turn to the side. Dead ahead the Verrettis boat bounced and settled as it hit the water, righted by its encounter with the guard boat, severely dented but clearly not too injured to flee.

Roxanne cackled happily as her sons let out a triumphant whoop and she accelerated, swerving away from the sandbars again.

Galen tried to punch the throttle, but the engine choked and sputtered as they shifted lower, taking on water faster now. There was no way they were going to stop the Verrettis. The boat wouldn't go anywhere but down.

That high-pitched whine rent the night as the cigarette boat bore down on the Verrettis, its black color blending with the night. Galen could hardly see it against the dark waves, but given how quickly Roxanne had turned again toward the sandbars, it must have been nearly upon them.

The bandits' boat hit the next sandbar hard enough to go airborne again, this time flying flat enough to slam into the sea and keep going, except that the sea gave way to a wider sandbar. Their boat hit the submerged island with a sickening crunch, skidded across the thin film of water, shedding speed as it came to rest high on the beach of the island itself.

The cig boat sailed past, slowed, whipped around in the open sea and turned back.

Ruby tucked her arm around his waist as their shattered

craft sank lower in the water. The sandbar was still one long swim away. "Can you swim for it? We're almost sunk."

Galen cringed at the thought but knew he wouldn't have any choice. The three helicopters had landed encircling the Verrettis' boat, and from the sounds of it, the swarm of soldiers had quickly apprehended them all.

"Need a hand?" A voice called over the hum of a boat motor.

It took Galen just a moment to recognize Rocco's accent. In that time the bounty hunter pulled the cigarette boat even with the sinking vessel, stilling to a stop and stretching out a beefy hand toward them.

"Oh, thank God." Ruby's teeth stopped chattering just long enough for her to whisper the grateful prayer.

"Thank God, indeed." Rocco grinned as he helped her aboard, gesturing with his other hand toward the sky, to God in heaven, who had helped them. "Thank God for the helicopter or I wouldn't have found you, and thank God I caught up to you when I did." He hoisted Galen onto his boat—a painful process, but Galen wasn't about to complain.

"You're a Christian?" he asked the bounty hunter, surprised.

"Why else do you think I attended worship at the cathedral on Sunday?" Rocco left the two of them shivering on the bench seat as he trolled toward the beach, dropped an anchor and hopped out onto the sand.

The moonlight spilled across the white sand, creating a silvery backdrop for the chaos surrounding the boat. To Galen's relief, the soldiers loaded the cuffed Verrettis onto helicopters while two bulldogs scampered around their feet, barking madly but otherwise appearing unharmed.

A soldier pulled a bulky bag from a storage compartment. Galen recognized the man from his days in the army—Titus, who he'd heard Prince Alec thank for saving his life earlier that summer. Titus opened the bag and his eyes widened as he pulled out a tiara, which glittered in the moonlight. He gasped, marveled for a moment at what he'd found, then put it right back in the bag and carried the whole thing over to the awaiting helicopter.

Rocco leaped off the boat as two soldiers carried away two more bags. A moment later the bounty hunter hurried back toward his boat with something tucked under his arm.

He grinned as he boarded, extending the laptop computer he'd retrieved toward them. "Don't want to get this wet, but you'll want to keep it, Ruby."

"The evidence." Ruby's voice cracked as though she might weep. "It will prove the Verrettis sabotaged Tate Jewelry."

"Don't know that it will change their punishment any— they should all get multiple life sentences for all the guards they've shot in their heists—but your folks can sue for damages. The Verrettis can afford to pay."

"Thank you." Ruby began to cry in earnest, still shivering as she huddled close in Galen's arms. "Keep it dry."

"That I will. Let's get you both back to the mainland, shall we?" Rocco lifted the seat in front of them, pulled out a folded bundle, tucked the laptop securely in the space and closed the seat. He tossed them the blanket. "Only one I've got, sorry. You'll have to share."

While the bounty hunter got the boat turned around, Ruby unfurled the blanket and tucked it around them.

"Are you doing okay? I know you've got to be in pain."

While he couldn't deny that his injuries were furious about the jarring boat ride, the crash and the cold, Galen honestly didn't mind. "I'm with you. We recovered the crown jewels. Everything is good." Still, he winced as Rocco accelerated, the force aggravating the throbbing muscles in his back.

"You're in pain." Ruby called his bluff. "What can I do to help you?"

Galen didn't have to think very long. "Kiss me?"

She did—a sweet, tender kiss that made his pain seem even less important.

"Better?" she asked as she met his eyes.

He grimaced as the boat slammed into a series of waves.

"Sorry," Rocco called back.

"What else can I do?" she whispered.

"Stay in Lydia?"

As the boat picked up speed and sped through the night, Ruby closed her eyes as Galen spoke the question she'd feared he might ask her. She was supposed to return to the U.S. and help her parents run the stores. But with the evidence on the laptop, and the Verrettis behind bars, her parents wouldn't need her help. In fact, if the wedding jewelry replicas continued to sell as well as the numbers she'd glimpsed on Vince's laptop, her parents would be able to retire comfortably. Although, without the meddling Verrettis making their business the bane of their lives, her parents might find they'd enjoy running the stores again.

Either way, Ruby no longer had to fear the temptation to stay in Lydia with the man she loved. Except for the captain's warning that if Galen became involved with her, he'd lose his job.

She nuzzled close to him so he could hear her clearly over the roar of the powerful boat motor.

"What about your job? Captain Selini said—"

"Selini said that if I kept the crown jewels safe, I wouldn't have to worry about my job."

"Does that mean—" Hope rose inside her.

He turned slightly and met her eyes. "I love you, Ruby. I've loved you since that very first summer."

Happiness welled up inside of her. "I've loved you that long, too, Galen."

"I love you more and more every minute. Marry me?"

"You mean it?"

His eyebrows knit in the middle, the infinitely cute expression she could never resist. "I don't have a ring like the jewelry you're used to—"

"I don't care. It's just jewelry, Galen. When the Verrettis were ready to shoot us, all I could think was that none of those jewels, not even all the crown jewels together, were worth your life. I don't want a ring, Galen."

"You don't?" He looked slightly concerned.

She hurried to clarify. "I want you."

"You'll marry me, even if it means staying in Lydia?"

"Especially if it means staying in Lydia. I love this kingdom, I love the people here. I hated leaving every summer. It almost made me scared to come back again, because I knew how much it would hurt to leave. But now I don't have to leave to save the stores. The evidence against the Verrettis will do that. I'm free to stay." She pulled closer to him, wanting so much to kiss him. But she had something she had to say first.

"So, you'll marry me?" Galen's eyes twinkled in the starlight.

"Yes." She kissed him until the warmth in her heart had chased away the cold of the night. At the sound of helicopters above, she looked up in time to see two of the three army copters headed back to Sardis. The third, no doubt, had stayed behind to secure the scene of the wreck.

Ruby leaned back beside Galen as the copters disappeared in the direction of the city. She looked up at the sky. "Look at the stars twinkling like a billion jewels."

"Isn't it sad that the Verrettis hurt so many people stealing jewels, when God gives us the stars for free?" Galen mused beside her.

"It's so sad," Ruby agreed. "I love jewelry, but not even Stasi's designs can compare with God's handiwork."

"You've got that right." Galen cupped her cheek in his hand, gazing into her eyes and smiling. "You're more precious to God than all the stars, more precious than all the jewelry in the world. I love you."

Ruby snuggled close to Galen until the twinkling lights of Sardis spread before them like gems in a city of gold. The marina stretched out its fingers to welcome them home, and Ruby sat up straighter when she saw figures approaching down the dock.

"Stasi?" Ruby gasped when she saw her friend, her bridesmaid's gown half covered by Kirk's tuxedo jacket, concern on her face as she watched the approaching boat.

"Ruby? Are you okay?" the princess called out.

"We're fine. What are you doing out here?"

"What am I doing? You guys recovered the crown jewels, you were nearly shot and drowned and—and something about a boat crash—"

Kirk chuckled and pulled his fiancée into a hug. "We talked to your brothers, Galen. They said you were quite the hero."

Distracted, Ruby almost didn't recognize the third figure until he stooped to grab the line Rocco tossed him, pulling the boat closer to shore.

"Good work, Harris." Captain Selini seemed to bow as he bent to tie the boat securely to the pier. "All the crown jewels have been accounted for."

"You've already gone through them?" Ruby felt amazed.

"They came in on the helicopter. I went through them myself." Stasi beamed. "They're all there—not one of them is missing."

"I'm afraid I wrecked the boat," Galen confessed, easing to stand up as Ruby helped him.

"From what the soldiers have told me, the Verrettis did that." Captain Selini extended a hand and helped them step ashore. "The stolen jewels have been accounted for. You saved everything, including the reputation of the royal guard—and my job."

Ruby's heart swelled with pride.

"Sir." Galen spoke in a steady voice. "You were worried about the royal guard getting a reputation. I might be making matters worse." He turned from his superior officer and smiled at Ruby.

"Yes, that." The captain cleared his throat. "I've been chatting with Her Royal Highness while we waited for you to arrive. She confessed to an attempt at matchmaking."

Stasi giggled behind him. "*Four years,* you guys. It's taken me four years trying to get you two together."

"You what?" Ruby took a step back and nearly fell in the water, but Galen had a tight hold on her arm and saved her. "Matchmaking? On purpose? Why?"

"Because I saw the way you looked at each other." Stasi grinned. "And because I figured, if you and Galen got together, even after we graduated and I moved back to Lydia, I wouldn't have to say goodbye to my best friend." Stasi reached out to hug her.

"I'm soaking wet." Ruby shook her head.

Stasi looked down at her impeccable gown. "Fine, then. Hug Galen. He's already wet."

But Galen looked at his captain. "With your permission, sir."

"The princess outranks me. She gave the order."

Galen pulled Ruby into his arms and the captain continued. "And she insists I need to promote you. I told her it might be awkward if you rank above your brothers."

"It might be awkward." Galen grinned. "But I think I could get used to it."

And then, to Ruby's joy, he didn't just hug her. He kissed her tenderly—and she happily kissed him back.

* * * * *

Dear Reader,

> *The decrees of the Lord...are more precious than gold.—Psalm 19:9, 10*

The crown jewels of Lydia are precious and infinitely valuable, but Galen Harris believes that a single Ruby is infinitely more valuable. Where does he get this wild notion? Isaiah chapter 40 tells us just how precious we are in God's sight.

God calls forth the stars by name. Though there are billions of stars in the heavens, God knows not one of them is missing. Though nations rise and fall, and generations come and go, God's love for His people never fails. In His unfathomable love, He considers us far more precious than the stars, more beloved than all the jewels of the earth.

Do you believe God loves you this much? He does. Hold tight to God's love and let Him keep track of everything else. He holds the stars in their places. When God is the guardian of our lives, we find every detail is accounted for. Not one of them is missing.

I hope you enjoyed this story of love and suspense. The royal guards of Lydia have more adventures awaiting them. And as you may have guessed, the Lydian kingdom has a history rich with love and adventure. For more information on my other books set in Lydia, visit my website at www.rachellemccalla.com.

Blessings,

Rachelle

Questions for Discussion

1. Galen doesn't hesitate to leave his post to save Ruby from her attacker, though his captain reprimands him for his decision. What do you think Galen should have done? Do you think Captain Selini was being unreasonable?

2. Ruby loves the kingdom of Lydia and finds it difficult to leave at the end of every summer. Leaving Galen is doubly hard. Do you agree with her initial plan to avoid him in order to prevent the pain of being separated from him again? Have you ever avoided someone or something you enjoyed so that you wouldn't feel the loss later?

3. The betrayals of the former head of the royal guard have tarnished the guards' reputation. Galen wants to put things right, but many obstacles block his efforts. How do you react to the hurdles between you and your goals? How does Galen respond?

4. Tate Jewelry has been having difficulties. Ruby feels it's her duty to return to the United States to save her parents' business, even though she longs to stay in Lydia. Do you agree with Ruby's sense of obligation? What parts of your life do you stick to out of a sense of duty? Where does your heart call you to be? How can we know God's plans?

5. Galen's older brothers have always given him a hard time and he feels like he'll never measure up to them. As you get to know his brothers, what do you learn about their relationship? Was Galen's assessment accurate? How do his brothers really feel about Galen? Why do you think they treat him the way they do?

6. Do the Harris brothers' interactions remind you of any relationships in your life? Do you treat anyone the way Galen's brothers treat him? What things can you do or say to improve your relationships with those close to you?

7. Ruby, Stasi and the guards have a difficult time figuring out what the bandits are really after—the replica designs or the crown jewels. Which do you think is more valuable? Why? What are the most valuable things in your life, and what do you think God values most about you? How can you better align your values with God's values?

8. The bandits repeatedly jam the guards' communication system. How does this complicate the guards' ability to do their jobs? Why do the guards need to be able to communicate with each other and their superior officer? Have you ever felt that the lines of communication were jammed between you and those you live and work with? How can you clear things up? How are the lines of communication between you and God?

9. Rocco Federico Luciano Salvatore is tough and imposing, and his presence in Lydia seems suspicious. In light of all Ruby has experienced, she would seem to have every reason for picking him out of a lineup and making sure he stays behind bars where he can't hurt her. Yet Ruby hesitates to do so. What might you have done in her shoes? How did it all work out? What do you think of Rocco?

10. Ruby dated a man she didn't really like in hopes of pleasing her parents. Once she got to know Galen, however, she realized what real love feels like. Have you ever been involved with someone who makes you miserable? Why did you stay with that person?

11. Ruby's father blamed her for the failure of his business, and claims she betrayed their family. In an effort to restore their trust, Ruby puts her own happiness on hold. What do you think about the choices Ruby has made? Does Ruby honor her parents through her choices? How do you feel about the level of influence Ruby's parents have in her life?

12. Galen and Ruby are held, bound and beaten, deep in the engine room of the bandits' yacht. They have little reason to feel any hope in the deep darkness. Have you ever felt beaten and bound by your circumstances? Have you ever searched for a source of light, a way out and found none? Where did you find hope?

13. Galen makes the difficult decision to let the bandits have access to the crown jewels in order to save Ruby's life, though he knows it will likely cost him his job and his brothers' respect. Though gold and jewels are precious, the Bible says wisdom is more precious (see Proverbs, chapters 3 and 8, and Job, chapter 28). Do you think Galen made a wise decision? Where does wisdom come from, according to Proverbs and Job?

14. Matthew 6:19–21 (NIV) tells us, "Do not store up for yourselves treasures on earth, where moths and vermin destroy, and where thieves break in and steal. But store up for yourselves treasures in heaven, where moths and vermin do not destroy, and where thieves do not break in and steal. For where your treasure is, there your heart will be also." How do these verses apply to Galen and Ruby's story? How do they apply in your life?

15. Galen shares Isaiah 40:26 with Ruby, comparing God's concern for the stars with God's concern for people. We

know God keeps track of every detail of the universe—
how much more, then, does God care about the details of
our lives? Do you believe God loves you and cares about
you this much? How does that belief influence your life?

(

REQUEST YOUR FREE BOOKS!

2 FREE RIVETING INSPIRATIONAL NOVELS
PLUS 2 FREE MYSTERY GIFTS

Love Inspired
SUSPENSE

YES! Please send me 2 FREE Love Inspired® Suspense novels and my 2 FREE mystery gifts (gifts are worth about $10). After receiving them, if I don't wish to receive any more books, I can return the shipping statement marked "cancel." If I don't cancel, I will receive 4 brand-new novels every month and be billed just $4.74 per book in the U.S. or $5.24 per book in Canada. That's a savings of at least 21% off the cover price. It's quite a bargain! Shipping and handling is just 50¢ per book in the U.S. and 75¢ per book in Canada.* I understand that accepting the 2 free books and gifts places me under no obligation to buy anything. I can always return a shipment and cancel at any time. Even if I never buy another book, the two free books and gifts are mine to keep forever.

123/323 IDN F5AC

Name	(PLEASE PRINT)	
Address		Apt. #
City	State/Prov.	Zip/Postal Code

Signature (if under 18, a parent or guardian must sign)

Mail to the Harlequin® Reader Service:
IN U.S.A.: P.O. Box 1867, Buffalo, NY 14240-1867
IN CANADA: P.O. Box 609, Fort Erie, Ontario L2A 5X3

**Are you a current subscriber to Love Inspired Suspense books and want to receive the larger-print edition?
Call 1-800-873-8635 or visit www.ReaderService.com.**

* Terms and prices subject to change without notice. Prices do not include applicable taxes. Sales tax applicable in N.Y. Canadian residents will be charged applicable taxes. Offer not valid in Quebec. This offer is limited to one order per household. Not valid for current subscribers to Love Inspired Suspense books. All orders subject to credit approval. Credit or debit balances in a customer's account(s) may be offset by any other outstanding balance owed by or to the customer. Please allow 4 to 6 weeks for delivery. Offer available while quantities last.

Your Privacy—The Harlequin® Reader Service is committed to protecting your privacy. Our Privacy Policy is available online at www.ReaderService.com or upon request from the Harlequin Reader Service.
We make a portion of our mailing list available to reputable third parties that offer products we believe may interest you. If you prefer that we not exchange your name with third parties, or if you wish to clarify or modify your communication preferences, please visit us at www.ReaderService.com/consumerchoice or write to us at Harlequin Reader Service Preference Service, P.O. Box 9062, Buffalo, NY 14269. Include your complete name and address.

LIS13R

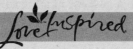
He took up her whole office.

At least that's how it felt to Melissa Sweeney.

Brian Montclair sat in the chair across from her, his arms folded over his chest, his entire demeanor screaming "get me out of here."

Tall with broad shoulders and arms filling out his button-down shirt rolled up at the sleeves, he looked more like a linebacker than a potential baker's assistant.

Which is what he might become if he took the job Melissa had to offer him.

Melissa held up the worn and dog-eared paper she had been given. It held a short list of potential candidates for the job at her bakery.

The rest of the names had been crossed off with comments written beside them. Unsuitable. Too old. Unable to be on their feet all day. Just had a baby. Nut allergy. Moved away.

This last comment appeared beside two of the eight names on her list, a sad commentary on the state of the town of Bygones.

When Melissa had received word of a mysterious

benefactor offering potential business owners incentive money to start up a business in the small town of Bygones, Kansas, she had immediately applied. All her life she had dreamed of starting up her own bakery. She had taken courses in baking, decorating, business management, all with an eye to someday living out the faint dream of owning her own business.

When she had been approved, she'd quit her job in St. Louis, packed up her few belongings and had come here. She felt as if her life had finally taken a good turn. However, in the past couple of weeks it had become apparent that she needed extra help.

She had received the list of potential hires from the Bygones Save Our Street Committee and was told to try each of them. Brian Montclair was on the list. At the bottom, but still on the list.

"The reason I called you here was to offer you a job," she said, trying to inject a note of enthusiasm into her voice. This had better work.

To find out if Melissa and Brian can help save the town of Bygones one cupcake at a time, pick up
THE BACHELOR BAKER
wherever Love Inspired books are sold.